URBAN PULP

Cover Design by DeChazier Pykel for Black-Marmalade Studio

Published by Over the Edge Books, Los Angeles

www.overtheedgebooks.com

Urban Pulp/TK Kimbro —1st ed.

ISBN 978-1-944082-14-7 (print), ISBN: 978-1-944082-15-4 (digital)

URBANPULP

1

ADHAN TO JHUMAH

Allah Hu Akbar!

I can hear the Adhan, which is the call of prayer from the Masjid. I'm about two blocks away from the Masjid as I drive into a gas station on Crenshaw and Adams. I'm almost out of gas and I don't have much time before Jummah service starts and this is the closest gas station I can go to without being late to service; that is the only reason why I would ever stop here.

The gas station is on the borderline of the Westside Gangsta Blood hood and the Westside Original Crip hood and has been called an open murder zone by the LAPD. This area has been really active lately for gang movement with the Crips showing a stronger presence over here. This is happening because of an ongoing war that the Westside Gangsta Bloods are involved in with the Westside Surs. The war keeps them busy on the outer borders of their hood, leaving this area open for vicious gang violence to take place.

The Westside Original Crips have been victimizing more people around here because of that distraction. I am fully aware of these facts, but because of this gas station's convenience and my short timeline, I decide to stop, fuel up, and get the hell out of here as quick as possible before anything happens.

I pull into the gas station in my red Range Rover with all my senses heightened. I am trying to pick up on anything that seems out of the ordinary to me. My 9mm Glock is lying on the floor of the passenger seat hidden from sight by my Quran and thobe.

I pull up to pump 5, but before I exit the car to put gas into it, I grab my gun and slip it into the waistband of my pants. I start pumping fuel into my car. I am looking around at everything that moves in the gas station parking lot and nothing alerts my attention. That is, until I glance to my right. I notice two teenagers moving towards me with boxes selling candy bars.

My gangster senses are telling me something is awry with these youngsters.

They aren't decked out in gang attire but they have a negative vibration to them. I slyly put one hand on the butt of my gun in my waistband and move in closer to my car as I pump my gas. I am totally on guard, ready and in a tactical position to defend myself if anything should transpire. As the teens move closer to the front of my car, one of them says, "Ay Mista, you wanna buy some candy from us?"

I immediately hang the gas pump up and reach into my pocket for a twenty dollar bill to give them. "Yeah, yeah, I think I have something for you here." I'm only doing this to size up the teens and see how they respond to my offering.

"Here you go, little homie. I don't need the candy though. You keep it."

As I move forward towards to the front of my Range Rover, one of them moves in to take the money and the other one walks to the right of the car around my passenger side.

My senses are on alert. I am preparing to move into defensive action the second I see any aggressive behavior on their part. My attention is focused on the juvenile in front of me, but I'm also trying to keep an eye on the one that moved around the passenger side of my car.

The teen closest to me extends his hand to take the twenty dollar bill from me and grabs my wrist in an effort to pull me in closer to him. He pulls out a small .38 revolver and points it at my face.

"Cuz, just give it up and we ain't gon' shoot you!"

My heart starts racing, but I think to myself, these dudes must be amateurs.

I now see that the other young thug is moving in towards me from behind, 'rounding my passenger side. I gotta think fast...

I grab the teen in front of me and twist his wrist with the gun in it towards him. I'm too quick for him, and he drops the gun on the ground between us. I reach into my waistband, pull out my 9mm Glock, and shoot him in his hand.

The kid lets out a painful scream! "Cuz, kill this nigga! He done shot me in my hand!"

The other teen behind me pulls out a small .25 caliber handgun and starts firing aimlessly in my direction.

Bullets fly by my head as I duck and grab wounded victim #1; pulling his frame up in front of me to use his body as a human shield.

Gunshots don't unnerve me, only gun wounds. This is part of being a gangster. It comes with the job. I retaliate with gunfire as I let off four shots over the right shoulder of my human shield.

Blood is all over my clothes from the teen I'm holding and he squirms in an effort to escape the gunfire coming from the front and back of him. The kid is shaking and squirming so bad that I have to do something or I might accidentally shoot myself.

I place the barrel of my pistol against his upper back and shoot him through his right shoulder in an effort to stop him from moving around so much. I grab him and we both fall back on the ground.

I am laying in wait for the other teen to move in closer.

As an amateur in this murder game, once he sees that gunfire from my direction, he moves in to see if I am dead and to check on the condition of his friend.

That decision will cost him his life.

He walks over with his gun in his hand and reaches for his bleeding friend's hand that is laying on top of me. We are as close to each other as I need him to be for a one-shot kill. As he cautiously leans down, I turn my head, open my eyes and look him directly in his eyes before I fire one shot to the head. Brain matter flies as the bullet pierces his skull.

I hear police sirens approaching and it will be a matter of moments before they arrive. I scutch from up under both bodies and hastily jump back into my Range Rover. I start the 4.6 engine and slam it in reverse so that no one inside the gas station can see my license plate and quickly move down Crenshaw in traffic.

I was only at the gas station for a total of five minutes. Five minutes is all it took to create a vicious murder scene. This is the pace of the insanity I deal with in my everyday life. Murder and death are the only constants that I have ever known in my entire life.

It's hard for me to even imagine that I was on my way to Friday prayer service to show my commitment towards Allah, and I am forced to shoot two teenagers who looked like they were no older then sixteen or seventeen years old.

I am now only one block away from the Masjid and park my car in an alley nearby. I look in the rear-view mirror and see blood all over my face, clothes and hands. I know I will not be able to enter the Masjid like this so I start taking my clothes off and wiping myself down with them to remove the blood off me.

After I am fairly clean enough, I change into my thobe, grab my Quran and walk down the block headed towards the Masjid. The car is registered in an old girlfriend's name so I will just leave it in the alley as it may become too hot for me to retrieve right now. Lightly jogging out the alley and around to the neighboring surface street, I finally make it to the parking lot of the Masjid. A feeling of calmness overcomes me. I am at my spiritual home of peace.

The sight of children playing, pregnant mothers, and wise elders make me feel safe. The Masjid is my sanctuary. It is the only place I have ever felt at peace and one with God. It provides me with the spiritual recharge and boost I need to see the world as something good and not just a place where people are murdered and killed.

Here at the house of the Lord, I am just brother Damu, fellow worshipper and follower of Allah. I am expected to do nothing any more or any less than any other Muslim that attends the Masjid. Even the comrades from the neighborhood who come to Jumah know that in the Masjid, we respect Allah and the Prophet Mohammed, peace be upon him and there is no evil brought here or done here.

I enter through the doors of the Masjid and take my shoes off and put them on the shoe rack. As I do so, I notice tiny blood specks on my shoes from the shootout. Damn! I say to myself as I head to the restroom to cleanse myself before Salat. I wash my hands, my feet, my face, and my hair with the water for absolution. I have to cleanse myself for my Lord and today I also need to make sure there are no traces of blood on me from the shootout. After I am cleansed, I go find a space to pray.

I face eastbound, lay out my cloth, and start my Salats. I move from standing up to kneeling at my waist to full prostration on my knees with my head to the ground. I now have totally surrendered to the will of Allah. I finally feel at peace and happy. Serenity has entered my total being and the events of earlier today seem as if they never occurred.

After I finish my prayer, I sit up with my legs folded under each other and start reading surahs from the Quran. The Imam starts Jumah and begins the Khutbah. As he reads from the Quran, I think to myself how I need to change and be more worthy of my Lord's love. I am not the maker of life yet I have taken life, time and time again with little remorse or apathy.

I know the principles of being good, yet I still continue to do wrong and ask my Lord for his forgiveness. I view my connection to Islam and what I do in life in the same way as the Italian Mob does when it comes to Catholicism and its involvement in crime. My faith is totally separate from my mode of operation, but the sins I commit always bear heavy on my soul

Islam is the only pure and good thing in my life. Even though I sin and do bad things, I am able to do righteous acts through my faith and religion to offset my negative actions in the streets. I helped build this Masjid with money that I accumulated in the streets. That's right, with blood money. I took something negative and made it into something positive.

I am only a man. And I am a contradiction.

I know this and I embrace it instead of acting as if I

am not. I am just trying to balance out the evil acts that I have committed with more genuine, positive acts of compassion before I return to my creator. Jumah service nears the end and we all make Salaat together. The last thing we all say in unison is Amin.

I am humbled as I am always after Jumah at how everyone comes together as ONE to worship ONE God. The brothers congregate around the Masjid after the service and engage in uplifting conversation or head outside to eat fresh halal chicken and halal lamb that is being prepared on the grill. I head over to the shoe rack to retrieve my shoes and head outside when I feel a hand touch my shoulder from the back.

"As Salam Alikum, brother Damu; How are you doing today Aki?"

It is the Imam.

I turn towards him and embrace him and say, "Walikum Salam Imam! All is well, Insha Allah it will continue to be!"

"Good to hear that young brother I wanted to make sure you are all right. I know Shaitan works overtime to distract a young Shaheed like yourself, but continue to put your faith in Allah and all will be good!"

There is something in his voice that alarms me. His tone is more cautionary than concerned.

"Shukran Imam and As Salam Alikum!"

"Walikum Salam, Damu."

The Imam leaves and I put my shoes on and head

outside.

As I step outside I see my Al Wazir Momar. Momar is my advisor in Islam. He was my Uncle Mo's best friend when I was growing up and used to come with my Uncle to visit me when I was incarcerated. Momar would always bring me Islamic literature and Halal food.

At one time in his life, he was the biggest drug dealer on the westside of Los Angeles. But that was in the early 90s, before he turned his life over to Islam. He has lived my struggle of being in the streets and trying to change through Islam. Momar is constantly on me to do better and fully commit to my religion.

"As Salam Alikum, Brother Damu. Did you study those hadiths I gave you?"

"Walikum Salam, Brother Momar, I haven't had time to read them yet, but I..."

He cuts me off in mid-sentence. "Damu, you had better make time, you hear? This is your soul we talking 'bout here, boy. You got time for all this other shit that don't mean nothin' but can't take no time out for your Lord. Bet yo' ass gon' have plenty uh time in the hellfire to study!"

Momar gives me tough love and most of the time I need and appreciate him for it, but today I have too much on my heart and mind to bear for his banter. "Look Momar, you're right, Aki, and I will get to it. I'm just moving fast right now."

My words trigger a rather odd look from Momar. I don't know what it is, maybe my words take him back to his time in the streets or maybe it's my delivery, but he moves in close to me and very sternly whispers in my ear, "Well, slow the fuck down then, Nigga, because you got blood on your thobe and it doesn't seem like YOU'RE bleedin' so it has to be somebody else's blood! Leave the Masjid NOW and ask your Lord for repentance, Damu!"

I move back from Momar and look down at my thobe and see a large blood spot on it. Now it makes sense, that's why the Imam was asking me if I was okay. I feel as though I have shamed the house of my Lord with my evil ways. I walk through the parking lot of the Masjid and head down Crenshaw.

It seems as though I can never rid myself of evil. When I arrive in the alley, there is a boot on my Range Rover. I walk right past it like it's not even there, pull out my cell phone, and call my homie and road dog Brazyiak to come pick me up.

2

Gangsta Rap or Rap Gangstas?

Today starts off like any typical day for J Loc. He is awakened at his Grandmother's house in Mid City Los Angeles by knocking at the front door. J Loc is disoriented from the previous night of revelry and debauchery and tries to re-gather his thoughts and composure. He slowly gets up and goes to see who is at the door.

J Loc looks out the peep-hole and carelessly unlocks and opens the steel bar door. It's his lil cousin Ray-Ray. As J Loc walks over to the couch and sits down, Ray-Ray boogies into the house and starts to discuss the neighborhood happenings with J Loc. Ray-Ray is only 14 years old, and what they call a "baby loc". Young, full of uncontrolled adrenalin, and totally consumed with the gangbang lifestyle. Ray-Ray looks up to J Loc who doesn't disappoint him when he breaks down his gangsterism.

"Nigga, I love this Mid City Westside Gangsta Crip life!! Tha' way I live life is to turn it all the way up, Ray-Ray; fuckin' as many of these beautiful hoes as I can, takin' whateva I want from these weak niggas, dumpin' on my enemies, and flaggin' fo' the set! I mean, I love it, cuz! Yo' big cuz'n has been the center piece for the hood since I was yo' age. I'm that nigga over here when it comes to Mid City Westside Gangsta Crips, and ain't nobody gon' tell you different unless they want a bullet in they muthafuckin dome!"

Ray-Ray is mesmerized and looks with admiration at his big cousin J Loc, totally engulfed in his bravado.

J Loc, at the young age of 19, is already a veteran in the West LA streets, but is on a head-on collision course with infamy and death. He is the third generation of his family to be involved with gang-banging and sees no other viable reality but to kill and rob on the streets of Los Angeles for his hood. He will never assimilate or move into mainstream society, even though his neighborhood has gone through a massive gentrification over the last five years. To J Loc, it would be a badge of honor to die in his neighborhood before he turns 21 years of age. He fails to see how sick and demented his thought process is, mainly because this is all he has ever seen and been privy to his entire life. He is the result of the post-civil rights era in Los Angeles and the payback to dreams deferred and unfulfilled. Simply put, he is America's nightmare – A Menace To Society.

Ray-Ray bounces out, headed to a "kick-back" across town. J Loc's phone rings, as he grabs it off the side table, he notices the caller ID says Lover Boy, his compadre from last night.

J Loc answers the phone and without even saying hello, goes right into dialogue about last night's antics. "Cuz, did I really fuck that Mexican bitch raw dog last night? I was so faded on that medical and Louie that I can barely rememba shit. That bitch did have a phat ass doe, that I do rememba cuz that's rare fo' a Mexican bitch to have ass like that. They be havin' tha crazy hip game and will have a nigga fooled from lookin' on tha front or side thinkin' they got dunk until you see that sloppy backside. Her shit was hella round and thick, that's all I can rememba. Good thing we was at the lil homie house down the block. Cuz, did I walk back home? I don't even remember!"

Lover Boy laughs. "Yeah, Cuz, you was on one last night, but J Loc we need to link up in about an hour, I got some high-powered Hollywood shit goin' on."

J Loc is laughing now. "Okay. Come scoop me in a few. I need to hop in the shower and get my gear togetha, cuz you know I can't be out with you looking raggedy."

J Loc moves through his room in his Grandmother's house and makes his way to the bathroom to shower and brush his teeth.

Lover Boy is the Mid City Westside Gangsta Crip connection to the Entertainment Industry and the Hollywood party scene. He has never been much of an active member of the set through acts of violence, but he had a mouthpiece and hustle to him which has always been of benefit to him and his set. Because of that hustle and his ability to talk, he is able to attract to him the right people at the right time. At this particular moment in time, he is rolling with Strapz, the biggest name in Gangsta rap and one of the highest selling rappers in history.

J Loc has always looked out for Lover Boy and Lover Boy has returned the favor bringing around lots of girls, connects to get in parties and concerts, and bringing around some big money players. Lover Boy is typical of many of the young westside gang members, his hood is going thru gentrification and he wasn't raised up living in a war zone like some of his older homies or the eastside counterparts. This has caused him and many like him to assimilate more into mainstream culture. He runs around Hollywood nightclubs and impresses silly young girls with his gangster swag as he brings the gang hustle to Hollywood and other areas around LA that aren't in the hood.

As to Strapz, he, too, is also a product of his environment. Born to a Belizean single mother in Los Angeles but raised in the mean streets of Brooklyn, Strapz has risen from being shot and serving prison time for murder to becoming one of the biggest names ever in rap, now at the top of the entertainment world. Strapz moves through the wicked streets that birthed him effortlessly. It is in these streets on the westside of Los Angeles that he met Lover Boy at a streetwear boutique on Pico Boulevard. Lover Boy is an impeccable dresser and always stays in the latest fashions. A young westside playa like Lover makes it his business to know all the store owners, stylists and general fashion forward people of Los Angeles who are based on the west side.

It is through one of these connections that he meets Strapz one day. At the initial meeting between the two, there is an immediate kinship as they both reveal a shared Belizean ancestry. Lover Boy also explains his connection to the Mid City Westside Gangsta Crips and how they run the westside as far as gang politics are concerned.

This definitely catches Strapz's attention and makes him want to bring Lover Boy into his crew.

In New York, Crips and Bloods have been active for the last fifteen years with varying degrees of effectiveness on the streets there, but gang activity in Los Angeles has been embedded in the street culture for over forty years. There is a big difference between the Los Angeles and New York gang culture. Strapz runs with the Crips in Brooklyn, but having a connect with a notorious Los Angeles Crip set like the Mid City Westside Gangsta Crips would take his gangster image over the top and provide him with a strong street affiliation to feel even more confident running around out in the LA streets.

Lover Boy sees this too and is wise enough to know that to keep Strapz intrigued in the mystique of his Crip ties, he must bring certain elements of it to Strapz but only the homies that he knows that will respect his connection to Strapz and not try to interfere with it. Lover Boy has little leverage of power in his neighborhood since he doesn't ride or actively gang-bang and because of that fact, most of his homies in his neighborhood might automatically make a gangster move on him to assert their prowess and strength in the gang. Lover Boy is aware of this and aligns himself solely under the dominion of J Loc who rules in their neighborhood, unchallenged by all.

J Loc also acknowledges this and leans on Lover Boy

whenever necessary to get whatever he needs from him. There is a balance that is very common and well documented on the streets of Los Angeles where violence and murder dictates who survives and who dies.

J Loc finished showering and is now getting dressed. While admiring himself in the mirror, J Loc is fixing his shit to fit comfortably and put on several of his gold chains. He's finally ready for the day. But not until he grabs for the accessory that every gangster needs to survive on the streets of Los Angeles, a large caliber handgun. J Loc doesn't grab one, but two .40 caliber handguns. He puts one in the front of his waistband and the other in his front pants pocket. He takes a final look in the mirror and straightens his weaponry out so that it doesn't bulge too much from under his shirt.

J Loc's iPhone vibrates again. It's Lover Boy is texting from outside of his grandmother's house and waiting for him. With a devilish smirk on his face, J Loc heads towards the front door ready to face another day in the concrete jungles of Los Angeles.

J Loc hops off the curb in front of his Grandmother's house and throws his neighborhood gang sign with his hands up to Lover Boy who is waiting for him in his car.

He then proudly proclaims to Lover Boy, "Lova Boy, is you M Dubbin' or what Cuz?"

Lover Boy shouts back to J Loc, "Nigga, it's M Dub or nothin' Cuz!"

J Loc gets into Lover Boy's Porsche. "This is that new Porsche Panamera, right?"

J Loc looks around at the car's slick interior and says to Lover Boy, "This shit is tha bidness right here, Loc!"

"Yeah, it is."

"I just copped it last night Cuz, thought I would surprise yo' ass wit' it when I rolled on tha set."

J Loc and Lover Boy both laugh and they head westbound to the Four Seasons Hotel in Beverly Hills.

The trip is only about ten minutes from J Loc's Grandmother's house. One of the things about the streets of Los Angeles that confuses people from out of town is how, especially on the westside, the gangsters are everywhere in the city. You will run into gangsters and bangers all over, from lower class apartments to high-rise condominiums. You can be in the lap of luxury one minute and one quick left turn and you are in the center of one gang's neighborhood and one quick right turn and you are in the middle of another gang's neighborhood. Danger is always imminent in these Los Angeles streets, no matter where you are located at in the city. There is absolute certainty that gangsters in every social economic environment are in the South-land, waiting to attack.

Lover Boy pulls his car up to the Four Seasons and stops at the valet, but before he and J Loc can even give the keys to the valet, they are spotted and surrounded by paparazzi. To the paparazzi, two Black guys pulling up in an expensive car to the Four Seasons in Beverly Hills can only be entertainers or athletes.

If only the paparazzi were aware that they are in the

presence of one of Los Angeles most violent gang leaders instead.

Cameras flash and videographers move in closer to capture images of the two as they prepare to step out of the brand-new Porsche Panamera. They bombard J Loc and Lover Boy with questions.

"Are you guys part of Strapz's entourage?"

"Is it true that Strapz is moving permanently to LA?"

"Where are you partying tonight?"

"Gimme a shot! Look over here!"

The scene is too much for J Loc. J Loc has watched this scene play out on TV all his life living in LA, but he has never been a participant of it until this moment. Lover Boy leans over to J Loc as they exit his car and with a devilish grin laughs, "Look at these fools, J Loc!"

J Loc mad-dogs the closest cameraman to him, "Cuz, if you don't get that muthafuckin camera out my face..." The cameraman looks like he is about to shit in his pants.

Lover Boy pulls J Loc away from the scene "Aye, we 'bout to roll up to the homie Strapz room, don't say shit to these camera niggas at all." J Loc looks confused as Lover Boy continues to explain to him what to do. "Don't trip on these niggas, the ones are always close by in this part of town. Just follow me homie, we good."

Lover Boy gives the keys to his car to the valet and rushes past the flashing bulbs, snapping cameras, and media assault. He motions for J Loc to follow him and he moves quickly into the hotel lobby.

J Loc follows suit as he walks in the cool calculated walk that an active gang member does to let the world know that he is gangbanging.

He turns to Lover Boy as they move through the lobby of the hotel and says, "Cuz, all this Hollywood shit is trey crazy fo' me, Loc!"

Lover Boy lets out a laugh at J Loc and responds, "Yeah, it is way extra. Now welcome to Hollywood."

The manager at the front desk in the lobby recognizes Lover Boy and signals for him to come closer. "Good day sir, Mr. Strapz is awaiting you and he told us to personally escort you up to his Penthouse suite upon your arrival."

A hotel worker steps from behind the front desk and shows J Loc and Lover Boy to the private elevator that leads to the Penthouse suite. As the elevator ascends, J Loc does his perpetual gangster surmise of the environment.

In his world, conflict and danger can erupt anywhere in a moment's notice and his survival depends on always making sure that he is totally aware of his surroundings, just in case something does happen, then he is prepared to deal with it in the best manner accordingly. He is way out of his typical element, but he has too much swag to let anybody know it.

The elevator door opens and J Loc and Lover Boy enter the palatial Penthouse suite before them. The entire massive floor of the hotel is being used by Strapz and his entourage and is buzzing with movement and activity as they arrive. The first thing that J Loc notices as he walks in are four heavily armed and gargantuan security guards on post in front of what has to be Strapz's master bedroom. The security guards immediately lock eyes to J Loc because of his large size and gangster demeanor and calculate possible trouble coming from him.

J Loc is looking at them, too.

He knows their next step will be to frisk him down for weapons or perform some type of security measure to assess his level of threat to them. He is not about to cooperate in any parts of that in the least.

He whispers into Lover Boy's ear, "You know I am double strapped up, right?"

Lover Boy whispers back, "Yeah, of course nigga, you always are."

"Lova Boy, I see these security niggas lookin' at me sideways and I know they gon' want me to lift my shit off, but I ain't takin' my heat off fo' nothin! I don't care if we in Beverly Hills or not, you know niggas die everywhere in Killa Cali and I gotta be ready! So you ready to get turnt up?"

But before Lover Boy can answer, J Loc the security guards quickly move in towards the both of them.

"Hold it right there fellas! Before you get any closer, we are going to need to frisk you guys before you enter into Mr. Strapz's suite."

J Loc squares off defiantly to the security. "Cuz, that ain't gon' happen. Imma tell y'all niggas straight up, I got heat and I ain't takin' it off fo' nobody, so if that's a problem then I guess we gon' have a problem then!"

Security is now moving defensively with their hands on their weapons, positioning themselves surrounding J Loc and Lover Boy in a tactical stance. J Loc is sizing up the security and seeing which one he should move in on first as they approach closer. Suddenly, Strapz comes out of his master bedroom at just the right moment.

He smiles at Lover Boy and says, "Cuz, that's how the M Dubs is doin' it?" Strapz lets out a hearty laugh and says to his security, "Security fallback, yo, these my LA Crip niggas right here, they good."

Security is not moving so Strapz raises his voice to let them know he is charge and says louder to them, "Y'all niggas ackin' like I don't pay y'all checks! I know they strapped up, it's cool though, fall back! An let 'em in."

Security backs down after hearing the seriousness in Strapz's voice and fall out of their attack positions, back into guard post.

J Loc walks past the four security guards scrunching his face with the sarcastic gangster grimace of while he flashes the gun in the front of his waistband and says to them, "Niggas, this Mid City Westside Gangsta muthafuckin' Crip!"

It is his way of letting them know that he is armed and ready to use his weapon. Strapz steps in front of his security and puts his arm around Lover Boy. He then leads Lover Boy and J Loc inside his cavernous master bedroom.

"Lova Boy, you know how to make one helluva entry

yo!"

Lover Boy slyly shoots back to Strapz, "Yeah, you know me, shinin' and Westsidin!" They both laugh. Lover Boy continues. "Strapz, this is my homie from the hood I been tellin' you 'bout: J Loc!"

Strapz directs his attention on J Loc. "So you the muthafuckin' man I been hearin' so much from Lover Boy 'bout, huh? So what's crackin' witcha, Cuz?"

J Loc automatically goes into his Mid City Westside Gangsta Crip mode and asserts his presence as an active gang leader. He looks Strapz directly in both his eyes and says, "Cuz, I'm M Dubbin, and bangin' like it's nothin'"!

Strapz extends his hand to J Loc and they exchange the Crip handshake.

"Cuz, where you 'sposed to be from?"

Strapz answers J Loc back, "I'm from Marcus Garvey Gangsta Crip, Cuz!"

He senses that J Loc is feeling him out to see what his gangster is really about. This is the same routine that most gangsters exchange with one another all over the country when they first meet, but Strapz does not know how much more different this evaluation procedure is in the streets of Los Angeles from New York.

In New York, the display and response to the question is more for machismo posturing than anything else.

That is not the case in LA.

The question and answer in the streets of LA are more of a feeler for a gangster to see if you will proudly claim your set to them or cower under their forced pressure. The wrong answer to the question can often have dire results out here.

J Loc gives Strapz a look of disbelief; he doesn't have much respect for off-brand Crip gangs.

"Is that right, Cuz? Well, this Mid City Westside Deuce Killa Gangsta Crip right here, Cuz!" J Loc raises his voice and hardens his stare on Strapz. "You say you a Gangsta Crip? Then you gotta be Deuce killin' then, right, my nigga?"

Strapz is immediately caught off guard, as he doesn't fully understand what J Loc is saying to him.

He tries to answer J Loc the best he can. "Naw Cuz, our shit a lil different on the eastside Loc. We don't have the same beefs you have. All Crips back home are unified togetha to kill whoever we got problems with, Latin Kings, Bloods, whoever!" Strapz continues, "Crips don't beef wit' Crips in New York, Cuz."

J Loc chuckles a bit to himself. To him, it is inconceivable to be a Gangsta Crip and not have beef with a Deuce Crip. "Well, y'all niggas is fucked up then, Cuz, and need to get y'all Gangsta Crip in line! Ain't no treaties out here with no Deuces, Cuz! Them niggas done killed trey many homies and dissed the set to be anythang but enemies fo' life. Deuces ain't shit but a bad mark on the Crip card and I make it my bidness to take them niggas off the turf one by one." Clearly angered, J Loc continues. "And if you gon' claim Gangsta Crip out here Cuz, you betta get wit' tha muthafuckin' program!"

Lover Boy looks uncomfortable and wonders if he fucked up bringing J Loc around his new meal ticket Strapz.

Strapz realizes that he has angered J Loc with his answer. He can look at his face and body language and see the visible signs of his anger. He wants to change the feeling in the room and bows down to J Loc and quickly admits his mistake. "That's what it is then, homie! Put me up on game. I want to get my politics right out here on these LA streets! I meant no disrespect at all, Cuz, I was just speakin' on how politics is back home with the C." As J Loc stares at him, Strapz continues, "I know a lot of our Crippin' ain't right, Cuz and that's why I got you and Lova Boy around so you can teach me. See shit the right way, homie."

Strapz is from the street, but the entertainment biz has made him soft and he wants that gangsta energy he is feeling from J Loc in his world.

J Loc feels this and knows that his position as a rider has been felt by Strapz.

He already let Strapz know that he will not tolerate anything that he feels as an infraction to his gangsters even in the slightest way from him so now he can bring down his intensity. But inside his head, J Loc sees a huge come up, with one of the biggest rappers in the game jocking him like that. "Yeah Cuz, we gon' getcha Gangsta Crip right... Deuce killa!"

Strapz likes what he has seen in J Loc. He watched him stand up to his security detail and confront him concerning the correct way of being a Crip. So many of the guys in Strapz crew are Yes Men and would never talk shit to him. Strapz is tired of having too many ass-kissers around him. As a pampered artist at the top of the entertainment industry, Strapz is used to people giving into his unbridled whims and demands; it feels good to him to see someone have the guts to put him in his place.

"Yo, y'all niggas just brought some realness back into my life, homie!" Strapz begins to open up to J Loc and Lover Boy. "It feels good to be around some real niggas again, ya feel me? All these Industry niggas is so fuckin' fake, even my security guards is fake. Everybody just around a nigga to get something of off me!"

Strapz suddenly stops talking and an idea comes into his mind. "Yo, I just gotta great idea!" He points at J Loc and says, "J Loc, I want you to be on my security team! I need to have that real "C" vibe with me at all times and I like how you stand up for what you believe in, Cuz!"

J Loc has never worked a job in his life. He can't even imagine what it even entails to work for someone other than the Mid City Westside Gangsta Crips. He is at a loss for words momentarily, then says, "Cuz, I ain't neva had no job in my life 'cept Crippin' so Imma have ta think on that, Loc."

"Yo, I hear you, J Loc, but I gotta promo run in a few days in tha Midwest for two weeks, yo, and I need you and Lova Boy to come fuck witcha Loc for a while on tha road."

Lover Boy and J Loc look at him.

"Everything is on me! Bitches, clothes, food, whateva, Cuz, just come "C" if you can fuck wit' me on this."

Lover Boy and J Loc now look at each other, taking in the amazing news that they have just heard from Strapz.

Lover Boy speaks first. "Come on J Loc, we gotta at least fuck wit' the homie fo' this quick O.T. run at least if nothin' at all!"

J Loc agrees with Lover Boy, still trying to be cool and not show how excited he really is. "Yeah, fuck it. I'm wit' it."

Strapz is grins big, "That's it then, Locos! Y'all niggas is rollin' wit' me."

Strapz is strutting around the Master bedroom suite talking and grabbing bags at the same time. He grabs a set of keys off a dresser. "We got to go celebrate Cuz! The first thing we 'bout to do is head out to my new crib in Malibu just the three of us and fuck with these groupie ass hoes I got from the Valley! J Loc, you gon' hold me down wit' tha heats and you gon' drive the whip. Y'all niggas ready?"

"Nigga, we stay ready. We M Dub Gangstas, homie!"

Strapz throws the Crip "C" hand sign in the air and all three exchange handshakes and head out of the master bedroom suite.

After they jump into Strapz's vehicle and get on the road, J Loc is still trying to soak in everything that has just happened to him in the last hour. Strapz, one of the most popular rappers in the world, has asked him to join his entourage as security and go on the road all expenses paid for two weeks.

Now Strapz wants J Loc to come on the road with

him immediately and is willing to do whatever it takes to get him to say yes to his offer including coaxing him with gorgeous groupies for sex at Strapz's new Malibu mansion where they are en route to now.

"Damn, I love the PCH!" Strapz screams out loud with half his body out of the sunroof of his Porsche while J Loc drives it up the PCH towards Malibu. J Loc loves driving up PCH too; it is one of the few things in life that brings him tranquility and a sense of calmness.

J Loc responds back to Strapz, "Yeah Cuz, I fucks with PCH. It's kinda far from the hood but I like to come over here and get away from it all. I got kicked out of every school in the Mid City area! Then niggas got bussed all the way out here from the M Dubs!"

Strapz laughs. "Shit, J Loc that shit sound like my school history."

"Exactly! Nigga I was hard on bustas and enemies in school and pressed a hard line. It's just the M Dub Gangsta Crip in a nigga!"

J Loc and Strapz both let out hearty laughs at what he just said. They move through Pacific Palisades' oceanfront views and the PCH's curves with the precision that only a foreign sports car can make. Lover Boy is trailing right behind them in Strapz's brand-new Maybach S63 Mercedes Benz.

Strapz settles back down in the Porsche after wildin' out thru the sunroof. He pulls out some weed and a swisher sweet from under his seat. "Yo, I'm 'bout to roll this swisher real quick, keep an eye out for one time"

Strapz quickly and expertly rolls the weed in the cigar and lights it...

After a few puffs, he becomes more relaxed and passes it to J Loc for a hit and says, "Yo, let me tell you somethin' Cuz, when I was locked up north in that cage, I used to dream about lookin' at tha Pacific and rollin' up tha coast like we doin' now! I bug out sometimes Cuz, just being out here in tha free world and able to smoke the best weed and feel tha fuckin' Pacific Ocean blow on me, yo, that's that Tupac shit right there, my nigga!"

J Loc hits the blunt and replies back, "Yeah that is some 'Pac type shit, I just neva fucked wit' dude like that doe, rolling with all those Bloods, I wasn't feeling that at all!"

They both laugh again as the weed and the weather put them further into good moods.

Strapz goes more in-depth on his past with J Loc. "Nigga, all this fame and money shit has happened so fast for me that sometimes I forget that I was locked up fo' a body facin' twenty wit' a L just three years ago. Niggas ain't knowin', but I was really in tha streets before I got on rappin', I murked this nigga in a robbery and them devils threw tha book at me, yo! I was already active in tha streets when I became a Crip. I didn't start loc'n 'til I came from Downstate prison to Elmira Upstate. Once I got up there, you either Bloodin' or you Crippin'. All my homies from my projects Marcus Garvey was trues so I got wit' 'em and joined the set. We changed tha whole program up-north cuz we was the first niggas to go at tha Bloods and Latin Kings hard body!"

He took a hit off the blunt and continued. "Shit, I got the name Strapz 'cuz I was always heated wit' them hammers!! That was my hood name. I been bustin' my ratchet since I wuz sixteen. I wuz really wit' tha bidness but once a nigga got on wit' this rap shit I had to fallback, yo. When you gettin' bread, as a young nigga, muthafuckas is always lookin' to start shit just so they can get a ticket offa you, lawsuits and shit, my first year in tha game I paid out one point five in lawsuits!"

J Loc looks astonished at the amount. "Damn Cuz, almost two tickets?"

Strapz continues hitting the blunt and then says, "Yeah nigga, I had to learn tha hard way about this music shit, but after losin' that bread I wised up and got security. You saw how quick they wuz on yo' ass, them niggas don't play that shit!"

"Well, if them security niggas is so official, why you wanna fuck wit' me then, Cuz?"

"Them niggas ain't got no heart tho, Loc, they just doin' they muthafuckin' job, but you, nigga, youse a rida, you gon' do it 'til you die, cuz you a rider! I need that homie protection and those security niggas don't know nothin' about that shit! Plus, I'm trying to be connected in these LA streets! I want to be able to roll the streets of LA knowing I'm down with the hardest click of niggaz out here!"

"I feel you on that, Cuz. If you the homie, then it's on wit' whoeva, howeva!"

"That's that shit I'm talkin' 'bout Loc, that fire in you; I need that around to keep me grounded and on point!"

"Well that's what it is then, Strapz, but you gots ta be careful wit' yo' Gangsta Crip out here, all that OT Crip shit don't mean shit out here in LA; we only trippin' on what we goin' thru in these streets Loc. You seen wit' me, then you catchin' all my enemies and all the hate that comes wit' that, Cuz. Is you ready fo' that, homie?"

"Cuz, I'm wit' it! Niggas been hatin' and tryin' to murk me since way back, yo. Ain't nuttin' new to me, I'm ready to go all out, J Loc!"

Strapz extends his hand out to J Loc and once again they exchange the Crip handshake to solidify their bond.

"On Crip, what's up with the BPB, Cuz? My old manager Supreme, his Pops is from there and he used to always speak on them niggas back home."

At the mere mention of a Blood neighborhood J Loc's facial expression changes. He scrawls his face and says, "Them niggas ain't shit to me, Cuz! We always at war wit' 'em. Tha main nigga over there, Damu, shot up a bunch of my OGs back in the day. I been gunnin' fo' that nigga fo' years. He runs wit' my worse fuckin' enemy this other nigga named Brazyiak from the Westside. Me and that nigga been beefin' since elementary. It's on sight wit' us two, Cuz!"

"Yo, that's crazy, J Loc! Damu is the nigga Supreme lil brotha. Me and that nigga Supreme fell out as soon as I started movin' big units. He was fuckin' wit' all the Bloods in Brooklyn and my Crippin' was causin' us problems."

"Fuck them niggaz, Cuz! Them niggas can miss me wit' all that shit, How far are we from your crib Strapz? A niggaz gotta piss..."

"Yeah, we gotta 'bout ten mo' minutes, Cuz."

"Cool, I'm ready to see what's up with them groupies you was talkin' about!"

"Yeah, we 'bout to give it to those bitches and then I'm gonna pack up for the promo run!"

"That's what it is, Loco. Let's get it crackin' on M Dubs!"

3

EASTSIDE MISSION

Blood, all my life, or at least all that I can remember, I been shootin' and killin' niggas!

It ain't shit for me to run up or walk up to a muthafucka and knock his meat straight out his fuckin' taco with tha thumper. I done seen niggas' brain meat danglin' out they skull and that shit, it didn't even faze me in the least bit.

I just look at that shit like one day niggas is gonna knock my shit off, so I might as well get as many niggas out here as I can before I leave this bitch from a nigga gettin' me.

It might sound demonic or devilish to you, but to me, it ain't shit but tha reality of tha life I lead Blood. It's just regular life to me in tha streets of LA, where tha strong live and the weak die. But I ain't no foul nigga. I mean, I believe in God and shit. I be hearing my big homie Damu talk that Allah shit and I respect that, but I ain't no Muslim My religion is Bloodin', straight up.

I live and I'm gon' die a Blood.

Hopefully before I die, I can make it up to God fo' all tha bad shit I have done in my life. If not, then fuck it, Blood, it is what it is! From dirt I came and from dirt I will go back to. I'm just thinkin' 'bout life and death right now Blood, because I got work to do on tha East-side for the set. Tha Mafia calls putting in work contract killing or murder for hire, but for me, it's just a part of who I am and what I do Blood. To tell you tha truth, chip or no chip, I would still lay niggas down because I like doin' tha shit. I enjoy it Blood. I just like tha muthafuckin rush of blowin' a busta head off wit' tha heat and gettin' away wit' it! The anticipation, the hunt, the escape. I love all that good shit Blood.

Now most niggas my age would rather go to the club and get some pussy and trick off they cheese on some hoes. Not me, tho! My dick get hard shootin' muthafuckas down! I get off the most from doin my gangster shit. Violence is like sex to me. Shit, it's even betta than fuckin' because once you get known for poppin' niggas' wigs out here, you gon' get way mo' respect for that shit then you would for mackin' a dumb bitch and fuckin' her. Anyway, my big homie Big Bick Back needs me to settle a score for him and he knows how the YG loves to ride fo' tha set. Big Bick Back is from tha East-side part of my hood and that's where I myself originated from.

I grew up under him, and he grew up under my Pops Big Brazy. I started tha West-side Gangsta Bloods when I moved to Mid City at thirteen as an extension of our hood, tha East-side Gangsta Bloods. I put work in for tha big homie from time to time to keep the lines open between tha East and tha West-side sets of our Hood. Plus, it keeps them grimy-ass Eastie niggas in check.

You gotta shoot a nigga all the time over there to show them niggas what's poppin' because they be hungrier than a muthafucka and will try to get at yo' ass fo' what you got, same gang or not. But by me bein' who I am and bein' known to kill a nigga in a minute, it lets them niggas know what time it is with me Blood!!! Niggas KNOW they gon' have a real heavy problem on their hands dealin' wit' me Blood!

But lately with tha Eses outmanning' the homies on tha East-side six to one, tha homies been gettin' massacred in tha streets over there heavy!! The Mexican and black gangs have been on the verge of an all out war and I'm down to do whatever for my set and help us survive under these odds. Plus killing some of these Eses helps spread tha message on what my homie Damu is tryin' to do gettin' this Blood Alliance thang off the ground, uniting all Bloods in the Bity under one bar togetha.

Since I ride for tha homie, I been gettin' ridas from different westside Blood hoods to chunk at tha Eses on the eastside with me on these lil missions I been doin'.

Shit been comin' out brackin'!!

We got tha Eses wonderin' what tha fuck is goin' on wit' all tha Bloods comin' togetha! With each mission done, niggas go back to their hoods and spread the word and it makes more niggas wanna ride with us in tha Blood Alliance against tha Eses. Niggas is so sick of takin' a backseat to the Eses in jail and on dope prices, it really ain't a hard ticket to sell on linkin' up to make shit betta fo' tha B side. As far as I am concerned we can kill every Ese in the bity! The braziest shit Blood is that my Mamma is Mexican, which makes me half Mexican! I ain't never claimed that side of me eva, I'm a muthafuckin' nigga Blood.

When bitches ask what I'm mixed with I always tell 'em I'm creole and my family from Louisiana.

It's a long story but I don't fuck with no Mexicans in no typa way at all. None.

Since we been gettin' it off on the eastside, the Mexican Mafia has turnt up the heat on the 13s city-wide against all the East-side Bloods and put out a green light.

So what! Fuck dem beaners! Niggas ain't scared of them and as long as I'm on tha streets with a heat, I ain't trippin' on shit. You gon' die when you 'sposed to die. I will get my brains blown out before I go to tha bounty or the pen and deal with them Ese politics and their bullshit programs.

We are dyin' on these streets Blood, that's just what it is! But I ain't dyin' before I whack this nigga for Big Bick Back. I'm comin' up on this nigga's house I'm 'sposed to wack. I got work to do. This is what I been waitin' fo'. And if you think I'm bullshitin' on what I do with tha strap? All I gotta say is watch tha news tonight and be what I do Blood, it should be a good show fo' ya.

4
ON THE TRACK

"I can't believe that my life has come to this! It's 1 a.m. and I'm on Century Boulevard at a cheap motel parked in front of a room while my girlfriend Cindy is sucking some fat guy's dick inside the room. This is all too surreal."

I'm really pimpin' this bitch.

I always joked about getting in the game and pulling money out of bitches but now I'm finally in this shit for real, ten toes down in this motherfucker turning out my college girlfriend!!

I knew from Day One that Cindy was a freak and would do anything I told her to do. Standing 5'9" feet tall, Cindy was the baddest white bitch I'd laid eyes on. With ocean blue eyes, long blonde hair, and measurements at 36dd, 24, 38, Cindy was a brickhouse, sturdy and built for fucking. That bitch loves Black dick and sucking any Black swipe she can get between her pink lips. That's just a fact. It never bothered me, in fact it turned me on and made me like the bitch more because I knew that I didn't have to be around her all the time and I could do my thing and she would understand that because she was busy out chasing dick for money.

See, I'm a fly young nigga!! I have never been in love with anything outside of loving myself. I have been like this my whole life. I'm the only child of a Black doctor and a Black lawyer; blame it on them. I'm tall, light-skinned, and blessed with my mom's soft delicate features and my pop's gift of gab and athleticism. I have always been the center of attention and a natural born leader.

My pop's side of the family is the Browns, a clan of gangsters straight out of Inglewood. My pop is the only Brown to ever finish college and become a professional. The rest of them niggas ain't shit.

I was able to always see through the Brown's side of my family what the street life had to offer. The first few years of my life were spent close to them living in Inglewood, but by the time I was seven, both of my parents' practices were doing extremely well and we moved to an exclusive community in Westchester. That's where I grew up in the lap of luxury.

I thrived in this environment and I loved every minute of it. Because of what I was exposed to while living in Inglewood, I knew how to adapt the mannerisms and attitude of the hood, but I had all the education and privilege of being raised in suburbia.

As an athletic nigga with striking good looks, money, and game, I have always had bitches on my dick. I knew I had bitches in pocket since I was in kindergarten. I have always played bitches for what I could get out of them and it was always in the back of my head to pimp them out, but with my basketball career moving towards the pros it was just an afterthought, until I was injured.

I was the Pac-10 All American Player of the Year my junior season in college. I was pegged as the best Center on the West Coast playing for Loyola Marymount University, and it was almost guaranteed that I would be one of the top ten draft picks in the country my senior year. I had recruiters from every team in the NBA scouting and courting me and I was eating that shit up.

I was a star in college. Doing whatever the fuck I wanted to do and whenever I wanted to, fucking three hoes at a time, daily. Wherever I walked on campus, I got pounds, hugs, and shout-outs. NBA scouts were renting me Lambos and Maybachs to drive around the city in and be "that nigga". And I was...

Then out of nowhere, it all came crashing down six months ago in the beginning of my senior year. I was playing a pick-up game at Venice Beach right before the season started. I was clowning some niggas on the court with my skills when I came down wrong after a crazy dunk and ripped my Achilles tendon.

As soon as I landed on the ground I could feel that something was terribly wrong with my ankle. I couldn't even stand up to walk and I had to call an ambulance to take me to Cedars-Sinai hospital. As the ambulance moved in the heavy westside traffic from Venice to Beverly Hills, all I could think about was this injury stopping my basketball career.

I was right.

The doctor at Cedars-Sinai immediately rushed me in for x-rays, which determined I had torn and basically destroyed my Achilles tendon. Even with reconstructive surgery, it would never be the same again. With the doctors' prognosis, almost immediately, my basketball career was over.

I was devastated. After my injury diagnosis, I fell into a deep depression and cut myself off from the world. I am man enough to admit that I lost my desire to live after everything that happened to me with my injury. My whole sense of who I was had been based on me playing ball and going on to play professional ball. It was hard for me to let that go at first, but me having a "I'm that nigga" attitude, I eventually came back to being the true player I am. Just in a different sport.

I had lost my career, but I hadn't lost my looks or my way with words. Throughout my whole ordeal, this bitch Cindy stayed down. Even tho' I treated her like shit. I would wild out and not call her or pay her any attention and she would still stay down with a nigga. She knew I had other bitches, and she still stayed down for a nigga!! I was depressed and didn't give a shit about getting any pussy or even getting my dick sucked tho. No matter how bad the bitch was! I had just lost my calling in life, the one thing that I felt I was destined to do.

But what's ironic about the whole thing, it was Cindy that was jocking me! So as I started coming out of my depression, I made the realization that pimpin' would be my light at the end of a dark tunnel.

One day while I was cussing out Cindy on the phone about stressing me over not spending enough time with her, it hit me! Out of nowhere, something just clicked in my head. The Pimp God planted that seed in my head and it became time to harvest my pimpin'!

I told that bitch Cindy on the phone right then and there that my love was different than anything that she will ever experience in her life. I told her that she would have to show me her love in a way that she had never shown to any man before.

She bit it hook line and sinker, and like magic, here we are on the track tonight with her blowing dicks to bring me my bread.

The first thing I am noticing about pimpin' on the track is that it is hella time consuming. If a nigga has low hoe tolerance, then this is not the gig for you, but if you stay down, I see that it's money to be made. I love this shit though. It is just me and my bitch getting' to the money!! At the end of the day, I never ran with a bunch of niggas because somebody was always hatin' and mad at my shine. Fuck 'em.

This is my lane and I love it.

■————————————————————■

Tony looks behind him into the rear-view mirror of his Range Rover and sees the door open to the motel room where Cindy has been blowing the balls of her first trick.

She has been texting Tony the entire time letting him know step by step her movements with the trick.

"Daddy, it only took five minutes for this trick to blow his load! He's on his way out of here."

Through the open door, Tony sees the balding, overweight real estate agent tucking his shirt tail into his pants as he exits the room and walks toward the stairs. Tony continues to watch the man as he descends down the stairs and quickly enter into his car. Tony's heart is pounding with both excitement and nervousness. He has finally entered the Pimp Game and turned Cindy into a real live prostitute. As if on cue, just as the trick exits the motel parking lot, Cindy texts for Tony to come up to the room. Tony jumps out the Range Rover, hits his car alarm, and walks up to the room to check on Cindy, and most importantly to receive his first cash bundle as a pimp. Cindy opens the door to the motel room and jumps into the arms of Tony.

Tony shrugs off her playful advances, pushes her to the side, extends his open hand and asks Cindy, "Bitch, where daddy's money at?" Cindy reaches into her bra and hands Tony three crinkled hundred dollar bills.

"Here you go, daddy, I got the money first just like you said to. Baby, I love you and I will do anything to make you happy!"

Tony looks at the folded bills in his hands and accepts the fact that he has become a full-fledged pimp.

As Tony delves into his thoughts of easy money with Cindy as his bitch, he quickly grabs her by the back of her head, pulling her hair forcefully and moves her in closer to him, his lips are to her ear so she can hear exactly what he has to say, "Yeah, bitch! You are gonna be my #1 bottom bitch! We are on our way to the big leagues, just you and me. Just play your position and stay in line and you and daddy gon' have the world!"

Cindy kisses Tony and replies, "Yes, daddy," as he releases her hair from his grasp. The two sit on the edge of the bed and accept the fact that they have crossed a threshold together in which there is no returning point. As they sit in silence, there is a knock on the door. Tony gets up and looks through the peephole of the door to see who is outside. This is his first time here in the motel; he doesn't know anyone and isn't expecting any visitors. Through the peephole, he eyeballs a short muscular black man dressed in a gaudy pink three-piece suit. Right then, Tony thinks to himself, "This nigga has to be a pimp."

Tony yells from his side of the door to the man on the other side knocking, "What's up?"

The short pimp answers back from the other side of the door, "Blood, they need you to move your Range Rover, you are double parked!"

Tony hears no anger or malice in the man's tone of voice but he did notice the man said Blood, which means he is either an active gang-banger or affiliated. This alerts Tony's suspicions that there may be a potential problem when he opens the door. He opens the door slowly not knowing exactly what to expect but preparing for anything.

The short, but stocky pimp greets him with a handshake and says, "What up. My name is Suga. I got at you because they called me from the motel office thinking that your Range Rover was mine since I'm usually posted over here." He continues speaking while looking Tony up and down. "That's the 2013 Range huh? You got that mothafucka lookin' saucy!"

"Yeah, I just copped it about a month ago. Good looking out tho! Imma move it right now".

Suga extends his hand to Tony again as a gesture while saying, "It's all good. If you don't mind, let me ask you, you a playa, huh?"

Tony beams with pride as Suga recognizes him as a fellow gentleman of leisure and says, "Most definitely homie, I'm out here breakin' my first bitch right now."

Suga's pimpin' instincts were right! He knew he smelled fresh meat and he goes right in on Tony for his soft shoe pimpin'. "So this is yo' first time on tha track wit' a bitch, huh? I could tell by the way you parked yo' shit youse a freshwater mack. Dis what I'm gon' do fo' you, young pimp, I'm gon' lace yo' gators on some thangs 'bout the game out chea' and the first thang you gon' need to do is move yo' shit to the backside of the muthafuckin' motel! You makin' it hotter than a South Central July 'round this mothafucka'. The ones gon' pull up on you wit' a brand new Range parked out front of dis raggedy ass muthafucka. Park in da back right next to mine, and then come holla at a pimp. I'm in room 304."

Suga turns and walks away with the swag and bravado of someone 7-feet tall.

Tony just stands in the doorway.

For the first few seconds, he doesn't say a word or make any movements. He is literally caught between the euphoria of turning out his first bitch and the nervousness of entering a world which he knows very little about.

But what Tony does know this as a former athlete: "Always stay on your toes and keep moving no matter what."

Tony closes the door behind him and heads down the stairs to his Range Rover. He chirps his alarm, hops in the driver seat, and revs up the V8 supercharged engine, moving swiftly through the parking lot and to the back of the motel. He spots Suga's Range and parks his right next to it.

Tony quickly hops out and walks back to the motel. He jots up to his room to give Cindy precise instructions before he makes his way up to room 304 to get some good game from Suga.

"Fix your hair bitch, get dressed, and do your make up. We got business tonight." Tony swipes at Cindy. "I'm going upstairs to holla at this dude Suga and when I get back I need you to be ready."

While playing with her hair, Cindy smiles and simply replies, "Yes, daddy."

Tony jolts upstairs anxious to hear what "game" Suga has to offer him. He arrives at 304. After a few knocks on the door, a waif blonde woman puffing on a black & mild answers. Barely cracking the door open, she mouths, "What you want?"

"I'm here to see Suga, bitch," Tony says in his best stomp down pimp tone.

She looks Tony up and down with nerve, then turns and asks Suga if he's welcome.

"Fa'sho bitch, that's my young playa potna, let 'em in!"

Tony walks into room and sees Suga and four more bitches. There's the blonde who opened the door, two brunettes, plus two black hoes, one light-skinned and the other dark-complected. They are all scantily clothed and sprawled over the hotel room attending to the needs of their pimp. Suga is laid out on the bed getting a pedicure by one of the black hoes and motions for Tony to pull up a chair next to his bed.

Suga is a very smooth and charismatic guy. He leans up from the bed with a smile on his face like a father greeting his son for the first time in years.

"I'm glad to see you came down here and wanted to get some of this good game from me, young pimpin'! See, a lot of these popcorn pimps, their ego wouldn't let 'em do it, but youse a smart young mack, I see the pimpin' in yo' eyes, you got it, I just want to provide you wit' some propa guidance!"

Tony listens intensely and says, "I want to be as true to the game as I can be with this pimpin', Suga!"

"I feel that, but you can't choose game, game gotta

choose you! As a matter of fact, let me tell you how I got in the game. But before I get into it, you drank playa punch, young pimp?"

With a confused look on his face, Tony says, "I don't even know what that is?"

"That's Moet Rose mixed wit' Hennessey, strictly fo' tha playas!"

"I'll fuck with the Rose, but it is too early for me to be drinkin' brown."

Suga points to one of his white hoes and without a word being spoken, one of the brunettes goes to the mini fridge and pulls out a bottle of Moet Rose. She fills 2 cups with ice and brings them over to Suga.

"Here you go, daddy!"

The hoe opens the Moet Rose bottle and pours Suga a full cup of champagne. Suga grabs the other cup and fills it before passing it to Tony.

"Okay, young pimp, now sip on this while I break down some game for you!" Suga leans back and smiles. "Pimpin, I was always good wit' bitches. I always had a gang bitches on me or around me even before tha game, but I was tryin' to be a gangsta. Robbin', shootin', sellin' dope, anything to keep me banked out. But any time I was away from tha homies, I was soakin' up game from tha playas out here on Century or up on Sunset in Hollywood. One day, on Yukon and 104th, you know, over by Morningside High, I see these cross-towns that I knew was outta bounds. They was trying to visit a little hood rat in the apartments over there. On they way up out the hood, they thought they was gonna smoke a coupe of the lil homies standing out, but before they could get off, I shot both of them niggas the fuck up. IPD was on the school campus and caught me wit' the gun and that was it, I was headed to County. I was facin' two charges of attempted murder. I sat in tha County for eleven months fightin' that shit. At nights, I couldn't even sleep, it was too much shit goin' on down there. I'd be up all night just thinkin', mostly 'bout if 'I ever got out, I wasn't never coming back to that muthafucka again!"

Tony sits enthralled by Suga's conversation. He nods in engagement.

"Then one night as I was lyin' on my bunk I had a visit. It was the Pimp God; he came to me in a vision and spoke to me on tha game. He spoke on how he had blessed me wit' tha gift-of-gab and the power of attraction over hoes and how I ignored his blessings. He told me if I gave up gangbangin' and dope sellin', and stayed true to tha game, he would get me out of jail and give me a stable of top-notch hoes."

"Now, I was confused, young pimp. I didn't want to leave tha streets and tha homies 'cuz that's all I knew, but at tha same time - niggas wasn't puttin' no money on my books, sendin' hoes to come visit me or even acceptin' my collect calls! I made a decision to go wit' tha game and get money outta bitch instead of bein' wit' a buncha broke niggas! Two days after my decision, tha Pimp God came thru fo' me and the State dropped the charges on me for lack of evidence!" Suga smiled big. "The niggaz I shot wouldn't testify. Now game recognize game because years later, one of them niggaz I shot became a playa out here. I had gotten the opportunity to tell him how he changed my life by not workin' wit' them people mayne; and I had to acknowledged him as a true playa before he even knocked a bitch because he was true to the game, even as a gangsta!"

Suga took a sip of his drink and continued. "See pimpin', ain't no hate in this game! True playas respect tha greatness in anotha playa, if a playa is mackin' harda then you, use him as a guideline on how to step yo' game up. Bitches and squares hate, but playas we congratulate, ya feel me? This game is all about how you respect it, if you do good by it, its gon' do good by you! You already doin' good for yourself by startin' off with that lil white bitch I seen you with. White pussy sells tha most because that's what them corporate white boys want. Niggas want that pink pussy too, but they don't spend for it, you feel me? Start your stable wit' tha pink toes and bring tha black bitches in later when your pimp hand is stronger. Black hoes is always gon' be a problem at some point. Pimpin' falls in line for a white hoe mind, they adapt better, pay better & give a nigga less problems!"

And at that moment, Suga leans up, pulls Tony close and in a light whisper says, "Look around here at my pimpin', young playa! None of my hoes has even looked you in tha face tha whole time you been in this room! They wouldn't let you in the door let alone pour that drank in yo' cup! Ya know why? Because I trained these bitches good!

They don't need to do nothin' wit' anotha nigga but suck him, fuck him, and get that money to bring it back to me! Is you listenin' to me, playa?"

"Hell yeah, I been soakin' up tha game. It is so much truth in what you been speaking that I'm just lettin' it marinate!"

Tony is buzzed from the champagne and he wants to go upstairs and let everything Suga has said to him marinate and resonate. He stands up from his chair and extends his hand out to Suga, "Playa, you have laced my shoes really tight! This drink got me goin' and I need to go upstairs and let it all marinate. Suga, mayne I really appreciate this and I want to come up here on the reg and keep gettin' this game from you!"

As Suga stand to his feet and obliges, he offers a few more words of encouragement to his new-found apprentice: "Young pimpin', I could go on fo' days about tha game, this is what I live fo'. You got tha game in ya or you wouldn't been able to get that snow bunny upstairs to trick fo' ya, but you gotta follow tha rules and regulations of tha game playa. That's somethin' these otha young pimps don't do? They renegadin' on hoes! They easin' up on they hoes and givin' up tha game. I gave you tha manuscript, now just run wit' it."

They both shake hands and Tony moves to make his way out the door, but before he can close the door behind him, Suga yells out, "And get you a pimp handle too wit' yo' cold ass hands!"

Tony shuts the door and heads back downstairs. As soon as he opens the door Cindy rushes towards him, wrapping her arms around his neck. "Are you okay? Tony, you were over there a really long time!"

Tony brushes Cindy away from him and falls in the bed. Lying on his back with both arms behind his head, Tony gazes at the ceiling and utters, "Yeah bitch, I'm good! I'm just gettin' my thoughts together!" He pauses. "And don't call me Tony no more, it's Cold Hand Tony or CHT from now on."

5

SLAUGHTER HOUSE
(KILLING PIGS)

Brazy and Damu agree to participate in a mission to kill a dirty cop as a way to solidify a connection to the leader of the biggest Blood Gang in the largest housing projects in Watts. Brazyiak seizes the contract killing as another opportunity to further his reputation as one of the most cold hearted killers on the streets of LA, while Damu uses the killing as another link in his plan to unify all the Blood sets in LA in one combined front to battle all Crips and the Mexican Mafia.

But instead of the mission bringing Damu closer to his vision of a citywide unified Blood alliance, it actually works to further separate the Bloods apart from one another.

"Look Blood, fuckin' with these Project niggas always gives me the chills, Damu! You know these niggas kill mo' Bloods than they do the Crips over here in Watts!"

"Brazyiak, Blood, I am well aware of the conditions over here with our comrades, but we are here to further strengthen the Blood Alliance and offer them an opportunity to join our organization."

"Yeah I guess, but don't forget that I am from ova here, Blood. These niggas and my hood get into it at least once a year. These niggas killed one of my big homies and I ain't feelin these niggas in no way Blood, to me they just some Crips in red if you ask me!"

"I know their history, I know everything they about, but we need the Watts Projects Bloods in the Blood Alliance, they are the biggest Blood hood in Los Angeles County and even with all their tainted history they still are a much respected Blood set. We need to do this, Blood!"

"Okay, but don't say I didn't warn you when these niggas do some foul shit!"

Damu and Brazyiak move off Central Avenue and drive inside the projects. The Wilkinson projects are one of the biggest low-income housing projects in LA. Built in the early 1950s, the projects consist of 20 single-story black and white brick buildings. It almost resembles an inner-city rehabilitation camp. But it is also known as one of the most notorious death traps for those not from the area. Growing up on the westside of LA, the projects are a culture shock for Brazyiak. Knowing this, Brazyiak pulls his .40cal pistols out, loads the clips, and tucks one in his hoodie and the other in the waistband of his pants.

Damu's 760 BWM is already drawing attention as they pull up to park. In the projects, anything that is not seen on the regular is cause for alert. Damu calls OG Big Red, he is the shotcaller for Watts Project Bloods.

"Blood, we are here in the back lot waiting for you,

homie!"

OG Big Red is a legend of the highest order in the streets of Los Angeles.

Standing 6'3" and a solid 300lbs of pure penitentiary grafted muscle, OG Big Red is physically imposing, but it's what he has done with his girth that has made him so feared. In the early 80s, OG Big Red was one of the first Bloods to attack Crips in the penitentiary and start a decade-long war that was only stopped because of the Bloods and Crips unifying in the prisons to fight the Surenos. He is said to have murdered ten Crips with his bare hands in the illegal prison fights in Corcoran. He has been shot over twenty times over the years. He is the physical personification of a gang-banger.

Damu looks out his car window and sees Big OG Red flanked by over fifty Watts P Bloods walking towards him.

As Damu and Brazyiak exit the car, they are surrounded.

"Watts up Blood! We finally got Damu on the east side! You finally ready to get yo' hands dirty in this eastside mud, huh, Blood?"

"Big OG Red, it is an honor on my part to meet such a reputable Blood warrior!"

"Gotdamn, homie, you speak hella propa! I didn't expect da trigga man from da LaBrea Crab killin's to talk like a professuh!"

All the Watts P Bloods start laughing. Brazyiak is getting nervous and looks at Damu for a sign of reassurance.

If he doesn't see it, Brazyiak will start shooting and roll the dice as a gangsta on his outcome.

Damu doesn't flinch. He prides his self on his ability to speak proper English; it is something that he mastered while he was locked up in YA. It is a reminder to him of where he was and where he never wants to go back. He lets the laughter die down so that everyone can hear what he says and then he speaks with the confidence of a killer, "Yeah, I taught myself how to speak proper English when I was incarcerated for those murders, Blood, but you know from my Uncle Mo exactly what my murder game is all about, don't you, OG Big Red?"

"Fa'sho, YG. Mo is my nigga. Blood let me know bout yo' trigga game and da streets speak on you, too, Blood. I just call it like I be it, Blood. You may be a cold killa but you still talk like a muthafuckin' insurance salesman!"

"We need to get up out dis lot doe fo' da Ones come through this bitch all up in our muthafuckin' bidness. Follow me ova here, Blood."

Big OG Red leads them to an apartment unit deep inside the projects. As they move through the project, it looks like a scene from the Pied Piper in the Ghetto as everyone follows the hulking OG Big Red.

Once inside the apartment, OG Big Red gets direct to the point. "Blood, I been hearin' 'bout da Blood Alliance and I ain't impressed on dat shit at all. Niggas ack like I wasn't one of da main factors wit' da UBN in da pen back in da day, Blood. I don't give a fuck about comin' togetha wit' no niggas, Blood or not. We got everythang we need ova here in da pjs. Outside of niggas comin' togetha unda da B, how can dis shit benefit Watts P B Bloods? Straight up, Blood."

Damu feels the tension and initial opposition from Big Red on joining the Blood Alliance, but he also knows that it's all about money and power.

"Look OG Big Red, I'm working on a connect to go over the Eses heads in Los Angeles and deal direct with tha cartels in Columbia for access to unlimited amounts of work. I will be able to get massive amounts of powder for the same tickets as the Mexican Mafia without the politics, but I am only offering the wholesale price to members of the Blood Alliance. If that is not reason enough for you to join, then I do not know what will be, Blood!"

Just as Damu figured... Big Red loosens up to the proposition.

"Blood, dat sound like somethin' I would be interested in, but we still gotta work some thangs out fo' da set get involved wit' da Blood Alliance. I don't do nothin' wit' nobody dat don't get they hands as dirty as mine, Blood. I told you earlier, Damu, you was gon' have to get yo' hands muddy ova here fuckin' wit' us on da east side!"

Brazyiak has been on edge and frustrated the entire time they have been in the projects. He has "mean mugged" in the direction of anyone who looks his way, and has kept a bodily position of a soldier ready for war. Brazyiak's anger is building up... He doesn't want the Watts Project Bloods in the Blood Alliance anyway, and he surely doesn't like how

OG Big Red has been talking to Damu. He has tried to be silent out of respect for Damu, but the gangsta in Brazyiak won't allow him to be quiet a minute longer. "Blood, what is you talkin' 'bout? You been up in here wolfin' on what you used to do back in tha day and how PB's don't need nobody. The homie is tryin' to link up all tha dogs to get money under one card, somethin' that y'all old niggas could never do right after of all tha crack and water niggas was smokin! You niggaz turned into smokers!!! Nigga, you know I'm Big Brazy, son Brazyiak from Westside Gangsta Bloods, and you used to smoke wit' my Pops! Blood, I'm tired of hearin' all this shit!! All this talk, when y'all niggaz ain't killin' nothin' in the streets but each other! So what up, Blood, is y'all in or out?"

The mood in the room is tense and as sour as a rancid orange. All the Watts Project Blood killers in the room are clutching their weapons and look at Big OG Big Red for the word to take action. Brazyiak's adrenalin is racing! He's pacing, chest poked out and his hands are on his pistols... He's ready for war and if he's gonna die, he'll die standing up.

Big OG Red speaks. "Blood, you just as Brazy as yo' daddy. Y'all lil niggas calm down. Calm down. Ain't nobody shootin' nobody. Blood, I like how you stood up fo' yours and I respect dat Blood, but I told y'all in order fo' us to get in dat card wit' y'all, Imma gon' need some shit done!"

Damu asks, "Well, what is it that you want done, OG Big Red?"

"I need this pig done out! He been fuckin' wit' our numba one money trap in da back lot, Blood. He comes thru, fucks wit' da YGs, takin' niggas' work, throwin' all kinda bullshit charges at niggas. H's been tryin' to get my PO to violate me and everythang. Da nigga is too hard in our biz, Blood, and we need him done. Da Ones know we police killahs so it's gotta be done far away from Watts. We need him chopped off tha clock when he is far as fuck away from here. I got all da nigga personal info from my young bitch at DMV. I just need y'all to handle that fo' me and come wit' them low tickets on da work and we all in da unit, Blood!"

Damu looks at Brazyiak. They both share an intense stare that words could never relate. Damu is looking for assurance in his decision. Brazyiak's eyes convey he is fully supportive of any move he makes.

"Okay, OG Big Red, we can handle that business for you, but if you try to back out or play anything foul, then you will feel the wrath of the whole Blood Alliance against Watts Projects Bloods. We will green light you niggas, and force y'all niggas to stay over here in this eastside forever!! The Alliance will give you niggas problems if you step anywhere outside your hood... you feel me?"

"Blood, I told you where I was at wit' it. Whateva gon' happen gon' happen. I gave my word as a Gangsta Blood and that's what it is!"

"Okay, then I will holla at you to get the information that I need on the murder biz so we can what we do, Blood!"

"Ok, then we good. I'm finna bick back wit' da lil homies and get loaded. Imma be waitin' on your call, Blood!"

"That's what it is, OG Big Red!"

The men depart and leave with the universal call of all bloods: "Soo Whoop!"

Brazyiak and Damu head towards the door of the apartment. Damu exits first, but as Brazyiak closes the door to the apartment he throws the Westside Gangsta Blood sign in the air as a sign of defiance to OG Big Red. It does not go unnoticed.

"Blood is out his muthafuckin' mind! We might have to kill dat lil nigga!"

Damu motions to Brazyiak. "C'mon Blood, let's get up out of here before these niggaz change their minds and try to murk us before we can even get out the projects."

Damu and Brazyiak jump into the 760 Beamer and smash out of the projects. They drive just one block down and park on 108st in Watts; across the street from the police department.

Damu is waiting to receive a text to let him know the name, license plate, and home address of the cop he has been asked to kill.

"So we gon' do this shit tonight, Blood?" asks Brazyiak.

Damu responds, "I mean, fuck it, we over here now, mightest well."

The eastside of South Central Los Angeles is overly depressing. It is a dark and grim reminder of how the

California Dream was deferred for generations of African Americans. It is the hole that Crips and Bloods crawled out of and spread across the United States of America.

Damu has always been ashamed and hated the Eastside of LA. To him it represents a blemish on what he sees as the endless possibilities that black people are capable of achieving in this day and age. He doesn't think that him coming from the westside makes him any better than the black people over here, it's just that he knows they can do better if they are given the chance. By agreeing to commit the murder he is planning, he knows in his mind he is giving the Watts Project Bloods an opportunity to join his citywide Blood Alliance, but honestly in his heart he does not know if it is really truly worth it.

A text comes into Damu's phone and he reads it. It is from OG Big Red's girlfriend at the DMV. The officer they are looking for is Deputy Alfred Oppenheimer. Deputy Oppenheimer has been on the force for five short years and is still considered a rookie by his fellow officers on the force. He's also not very threatening: standing only 5'8", he has red hair and blue eyes. Throughout high school, he was continuously bullied. As soon as he turned 21, he joined the force and now vows acts of revenge, using his badge as an opportunity to bully those just as he was.

"Looks like our lil pig lives in Simi Valley, and drives a grey Dodge Challenger. Aye Brazyiak write this license plate number down 'cuz I need to erase all this info off my phone like now!"

"Ok, what is it?"

"6KHD579."

"Okay, I got it... whoop!"

OG Big Red texted them when he works so they know he will be getting off at any time now. They wait and hope he heads to the freeway in the direction they are parked. After twenty minutes, they see a grey Challenger with the matching license plate number speed past them.

The hunt is on.

They follow behind him as he enters on the 105 westbound heading towards the 101 freeway north. There is an art to trailing people, especially police. Damu stays at least seven cars behind Officer Oppenheimer; he wants to blend in with moving traffic as much as possible. The ride is a long one taking over 45 minutes through the San Fernando Valley. Damu and Brazyiak are quiet the entire time. They are both formulating and reviewing their plan of attack on Officer Oppenheimer; they are killing a police officer in a lily white neighborhood and there can be no room for error.

Officer Oppenheimer moves from the 101 to the 118. They know he is getting ready to exit and head towards his house via surface streets. They follow him off the freeway, but let him go ahead of them at the off ramp. Damu has set his home address into his GPS. They decide on going by Officer Oppenheimer's residence in one hour. Right now they are going to Denny's for food.

■────────────────────────────────■

Two Grand Slams and one hour later...

Damu and Brazyiak drive by Oppenheimer's home and see his car outside. This is a routine they will do every three hours until nightfall. During one of the observation runs, they see Oppenheimer, his wife, and two small kids get into his wife's car and drive to the mall and grocery store. They follow and track their every movement.

Where other people would have sympathy or some type of compassion for Oppenheimer as a father and husband, Damu and Brazyiak just see a contradicting racist, brutal, corrupt, killin' cop. The more they see him in his habitat acting as if he is a normal citizen, the angrier they both get.

They have seen cops like Officer Oppenheimer their entire lives. Police officers have long terrorized the inner city communities and then drive off to the suburbs as if nothing ever happened. These cops act as if the lives they destroyed in the ghettos of Los Angeles do not matter, because to them, the people there do not matter, but tonight in Simi Valley there will be some South Central retribution!!

As night falls and the warm San Fernando winds blow through Oppenheimer's Simi Valley neighborhood, Oppenheimer is standing outside his house smoking a cigarette and standing between his lawn and driveway.

As he exhales a cloud of smoke from his mouth, there are five quick zip sounds. He immediately clutches his chest, and notices blood pouring through his shirt. Totally caught off guard and by surprise, Officer Oppenheimer falls to the ground while gasping for his last breath. He has taken five shots from a high-powered semiautomatic weapon equipped with a silencer. Blood starts massively flowing from his chest and covers the concrete like wet paint. As he lays clutching to his last seconds of life, a masked gunman approaches and delivers one last fatal shot to his dome.

As the night rises and mist falls in this quiet suburban neighborhood, no one has even noticed the quiet assassination of Officer Oppenheimer.

Damu, with his 760 BMW still running, is waiting as Brazyiak opens the door to get in. He calmly puts the car in gear and drive towards the 118 heading west back to LA.

"Blood, I hope you happy. I whacked that pig, and we got tha Watts PJ Bloods in tha Blood Alliance."

"It is not about being happy, Blood, it is about being strategic and what we did today will ensure that the Bloods are a factor in the streets for years to come."

"But is it worth it, Damu? Blood... was all this really worth it?"

Contemplating Brazyiak's question, Damu pauses then responds, "I would say yes Brazyiak, but honestly I don't even know."

6
O.T. Run

J Loc, Lover Boy, and Strapz get ready to hit the road on a quick promo tour of the Midwest. The itinerary takes them to Pittsburgh, Champaign, Chicago, and Minneapolis. While on the road, J Loc plans to show Strapz how to "get his Crip on" according to LA street codes.

As they get ready step on to the tour bus, overly excited, Strapz says to J Loc, "Cuz, you ain't gotta do nothin' but get on tha tour bus. I have everything covered, homie!"

"That's what it is, Cuz. Do you got stash spots to put my straps if we get pulled over?"

"Yeah, we got stash spots. I'll show you where they at."

"Aight, that's tha plan. So we hittin' tha whole Midwest, huh?" asks J Loc.

"We gon' cova tha whole Midwest on our big summer tour, but we goin' to pick up some quick shows now, hitting some grimy spots like Champaign, Chicago, Pittsburgh, and Minneapolis. We gon' do these shows, make some fast cash, fuck a few bitches, and we out."

"I'm ready for it, Cuz! I ain't never been that far-east in my life so I want to see what it is!"

"Dawg, you gon' love tha road, especially fuckin' wit' me. Lova Boy, I hope you ready?"

"Man, you know I am ready fo' it!! I been on tha east, down south and in tha Midwest already, I just haven't been on the road wit' a famous rapper and shit, it's usually wit' a buncha the homies from the hood!"

Strapz, J Loc, and Lover Boy all burst into laughter. They begin grabbing their luggage and moving it to the door. Just then, Strapz turns to Lover Boy and offers a bit of a proposition, "Lova Boy, I been thinkin', Cuz, I like the way you handle yourself as my hype man and I think I want to put you on my label."

"You fo' real, Cuz?"

"Hell yeah, Cuz, you got tha look and tha swagga of a platinum artist already, plus you official in tha streets. I just need to go ova everything wit' my lawyer and manager."

"On M-Dubs, Cuz you will not be sorry, Strapz!"

J Loc chuckles, "Look at lil Cuz, now you 'bout to turn into Kanye on niggas!"

"Naw, Cuz you know I been on my stay fresh shit way before this, Loc!"

The tour bus pulls up in front of Strapz's mansion. As the door swings open, a big burly black dude with a beard jumps off the bus. "Let's move y'all, we got a long drive ahead of us and we need to stay on schedule."

They all grab their bags and begin loading them in the lower baggage compartment of the tour bus.

"Aye Strapz, what up with the stash spot, homie?"

"Yeah, c'mon so I can show you."

Strapz leads J Loc to the gun stash in the floor of the tour bus.

"Yo, put tha heat in here Cuz, you good wit' it here."

"Okay, cool, but if shit get poppin', just clear tha path so I can get to my shit!"

The tour bus is state-of-the-art with every amenity that you can think of on board. The interior is plush!! A fridge with all the juice and soda you could want, cupboards full of snacks, and a fully stocked bar. The studio and master bed is in the rear of the bus. This will be Strapz's sleeping quarters for the entire trip. As he makes his way to the back of the bus, Strapz says, "Yo, I'm tired than a muthafucka, I'm goin' to rest for a minute. Y'all niggas can eat, smoke, or drink. Tha fridge and tha bar is stocked up!"

J Loc goes to the bar and grabs a bottle of Hennessey. He passes it to Lover Boy as they sit in the front-end of the bus. J Loc and Lover Boy look at each other in amazement. They try to contain their excitement as they can't believe what is happening to them and how lucky they are.

J Loc states, "Cuz, I sho' wish Big Bo Peep wuz here to "C" this shit we doin' now."

"Yeah, you know Cuz was tha first in tha hood to show niggas how to ball. He would have loved this tour bus!"

"I miss tha big homie, Lova Boy, even killin' as many Deuces as I can ain't never gon' fill that void!"

"I feel ya, Cuz, we lost a real one when big homie went down but it don't stop tha M Dubbin!"

"Hell naw, Cuz, ain't gon' stop tha M Dub!"

J Loc and Lover Boy give each other pounds in agreement while the tour bus heads down the hill from Strapz's crib, down PCH, and to the 10 headed eastbound.

This is the closest J Loc has ever come to a vacation is his life. He has never been outside of Los Angeles in his whole life. J Loc has always been surrounded with violence. It's all about murder, death, kill, homicide just to stay alive. And because of that, J Loc sleeps with one eye open and a gun under his pillow. Paranoia keeps J Loc on alert. There's a medical term for what people like J Loc are diagnosed with, it's called Urban Survival Syndrome. As the tour bus moves further outwards of Los Angeles, J Loc starts to feel content. Truth be told, J Loc is happy to leave the city and the responsibility of being who he is. With his mind at ease, J Loc falls into a deep sleep.

Hours pass by and J Loc awakes as the bus is passing through Arizona and approaching the New Mexico border. He stares outside the window at the foreign looking environment. J Loc just marvels at what he sees out the window, while everyone else is still sleeping. He smiles because no one can see him. No one can see him enjoy this new experience. J Loc ponders to himself, "This must be what it feels like to live outside of LA."

In the back of the tour bus, Strapz wakes up, rolls over, and reaches into a secret compartment under his bed. He wants to show Lover Boy and J Loc something.

"Yo Cuz, come here real quick, I want y'all niggas to

see this!'

Strapz pulls out a large velvet Crown Royal bag from the compartment and loosens the strings at the top to open it up. He pulls out a handful of glittery Cuban link chains and diamond pendants.

"These are my Strapz Squad chains, cuz, I want both you niggas to have one!"

Strapz untangles and passes the heavy diamond chains and pendants to them.

"Now you niggas lookin' like new money! What up? You niggas feelin' them shits or what?"

J Loc answers first putting his chain around his neck. "Hell yeah, Cuz, this shit gangsta movin', Cuz!"

J Loc jumps to his feet in excitement and is rubbing his palms together.

"Now before you niggas get too accustomed to the jewels, I gotta tell you what's up. Dem shits is what we call fugazi back home... it means that they fake!"

J Loc hops to his feet and immediately interrupts Strapz. "What you givin' us fake ass chains for? That ain't G fo' shit, my nigga!"

Strapz quickly darts back at J Loc, "Hold up. Let me put you on to some shit, J Loc. Plenty of rappers and athletes rock out wit' fugazi pieces when they are out. All these shits are duplicates of tha real pieces I got back home. I got my jewelry insured last year and my accountant had me make these pieces to use while I'm on tha road."

J Loc looks at Strapz in disbelief; he always thought

that gangsta rap was fake and this just confirms what he had been thinking all along. "I hear you Cuz, but I ain't fuckin' wit' nothin' but tha real, I don't do fake NOTHIN'! You can have this muthafucka back!"

Lover Boy is looking in the bathroom mirror adjusting the chains and his clothes and quickly states, "Shit, give it to me Cuz, I'll rock both of them shits! Tha bitches is gon be jukin' on a nigga as soon as we pull into town!"

Strapz reassures Lover Boy by stating, "Yo, on tha real Cuz, when we get back to L .A. I'm gon' lace y'all wit' tha real shits you heard!"

J Loc looks in disgust as Lover Boy plays dress up with the fake chains in the mirror. He reaches down to feel his 9mm in his waistband. At least he knows that's real.

J Loc thinks to hisself, "Well, fuck it. We still got another whole day before we get to Pittsburgh, Imma chill...."

■———————————————————————■

The tour bus finally pulls into its first stop in downtown Pittsburgh. After a full 24 hours on the tour bus, Strapz, J Loc, and Lover Boy are burnt!! The trip took a few more hours than expected, so they will head directly to the venue for sound check before they check into the hotel. As they pull into the parking lot of Club Fever, Strapz, J Loc, and Lover Boy exit the bus and head inside for sound check. Strapz and Lover Boy immediately approach the soundman, hand him the show CD, and ask for the mics. As they run thru the various show tunes, J Loc walks around the venue and runs into a small teenager standing at an exit door.

The teen asks J Loc, "Whadd up, Cuz? You wit' that fake ass Crip nigga Strapz?"

J Loc has never met an official out of town Crip. To him that is an oxymoron, but once you say Cuz to him, you have put yourself in the line of fire and you will be treated as a gangsta. Squared up in an original gangster stance, feet spread and arms folded, J Loc barks back at the youngster, "Cuz? What tha fuck you say to me, lil nigga? This muthafuckin' Mid City Westside Gangsta Crip! Nigga this Trey all day! I don't know want tha fuck you tawkin' 'bout, Cuz! This real muthafuckin' gangsta Crippin' right here!" J Loc moves in face to face to the teenager and asks, "Nigga is you Treyin' or Deuce'n', lil nigga?"

The kid has no idea what J Loc is speaking on. J Loc opens the door at the exit and pushes him out.

"Boy, if you don't get yo' country ass up outta here fo' I put hands on you, disrespectin' tha "C" wit' that bullshit OT Crippin! Get on, lil nigga!"

The youngster hangs his head as he walks away, but has a few choice words for J Loc before he does. "You ain't seen tha last of me, nigga! I'm comin' back wit' all my homies tonight! Homewood Crip, nigga!"

J Loc laughs and closes the door, "Yeah. Okay, lil nigga."

J Loc walks back thru the club and out the front door to the tour bus. Once inside he plops down and rolls a blunt. The rap world is too goofy for him.

Strapz and Lover Boy come back to the tour bus and J Loc passes them his blunt.

"Where'd you go, cuz?" asks Strapz.

"Cuz, I just got into wit' some off-brand lil Crip nigga a few minutes ago! Cuz, niggas Crippin' is so weird outside the turf, Cuz!"

Strapz hits the blunt and asks, "What hood did he say he was from, J Loc?"

"Some shit called Homewood Crip."

Strapz begins rubbin' his chin. "That's not good, Cuz, they tha deepest Crip set out here. They probably sent that lil nigga ova here to see how deep I was! I had a lil issue wit' a busta from their set last year out here!"

J Loc slams his closed fist on the table with authority. "Well that wuz last year, Cuz! I ain't trippin' on none of these off brands! If niggas want it, then they can get it, Cuz! These niggas ain't reppin' right anyway! You got yo' security and you gotta M Dub Gangsta movin'! It ain't shit to worry about, Cuz!"

Strapz finishes the blunt while Lover Boy is hyping himself up. This is a huge night for Lover Boy; this will be the first time he will be on stage in front of more then 100 people. The show tonight is sold out, with a crowd expected of almost 5,000. Strapz heads to the back to get ready for tonight's performance.

"We go on at 11:30, Cuz... so rest up and let's get ready to do this shit."

It seems like the entire black population of Pittsburgh

is at Club Fever tonight. All the d-boys and bad bitches from the city are in the spot tonight. The VIP is poppin'!! And the waitresses are busy steadily bringing ballers and their entourages buckets of champagne. It's 11:20pm and Strapz and Lover Boy are getting ready to hit the stage.

"Mic check, Mic check 1, 2 – 1, 2"

The crowd at Club Fever begin to roar in anticipation of Strapz hitting the stage. Lover Boy is getting the crowd hyped!!

"Y'all ready for Strapz to hit the fuckin' stage?"

The crowd responds with a thunderous "YEEAAAHHHH!"

Right then, the DJ drops Strapz hit single "Bang Yo' Hood". Strapz hit the stage and the crowd explodes!!

"If you up to no good, nigga, bang yo' hood, bang yo' hood, nigga bang yo' hood..."

J Loc and the security detail have taken positions around the perimeter of the stage as Strapz moves from side to side performing his hit song. Lover Boy is the perfect hype man to Strapz, accentuating at just the right moments his words and movements, it is hard to believe this is his first show performing with Strapz tonight. As Strapz continues with his hook heavy anthem, all the various hoods of Pittsburgh answer him back. But from the side of the stage, J Loc can see a mob of about twenty guys, pushing 'n shoving their way through the crowd towards the front of the stage.

Once the Homewood Crips align themselves along the front of the stage, they start throwing their gang set up and shouting "Homewood Crip" in unison and with reckless endangerment. Strapz and Lover Boy are moving around the stage and too busy enjoying themselves to see what's going on. But the security team and J Loc do. This infuriates J Loc and he moves to the front of the stage and defiantly throws the Mid City Gangsta Crip hood up right in their faces. The Homewood Gangstas in the crowd become even more agitated and begin screaming their hood even louder all while arousing the rest of the crowd.

J Loc has had enough. He has been bred to immediately react to a challenge, it doesn't matter if it's 20 to 1 or a confrontation with law enforcement, you handle your business as a gangster and let the chips fall where they may.

J Loc pulls his saggin' pants up and jumps off the stage and into the crowd, instantly throwing jabs with members of the Homewood Crips.

He knocks at least three of them out with a flurry of punches, but he is soon surrounded and attacked. As J Loc is sent to the ground, he scrambles to get ahold of his pistol, which is in his waistband. While being stomped & kicked, J Loc shouts out, "Y'all niggas got me fucked up, Cuz! This Deuce killin' Mid City Westside Gangsta Crips! But you niggas gon' know from now on to respect gangstas movin'!"

J Loc lets off 4 shots from his 40cal.

Blocka, blocka, blocka, blocka!!!!!!

As the gunshots ring out and the Homewood Crips run for cover, at least two people have been struck by the gunfire. The venue's main house lights come on and security rushes Strapz and Lover Boy off stage. J Loc jumps up, puts his gun back in his waistband and runs out of the back door of the venue. With the sound of sirens nearing, J Loc cautiously runs toward the tour bus, looking all around him to make sure no one is following him. As he reaches the tour bus, the door swings open and Strapz, Lover Boy, and the security team yell for J Loc, "Hurry up Cuz, get in, get in!"

As J Loc jumps onboard, the door swings closed behind him and the bus skretches through the back alley. J Loc moves to the center of the bus, again pacing, adrenaline pumping he moves towards Strapz and pushes up on him... "Here cuz, take this and put it in the stash... NOW!!"

Strapz moves towards the front of the bus and pulls the carpet back on the floor to expose the stash spot. He lifts up a wood panel and tosses the still smokin' pistol into the stash.

As the bus moves out of the vicinity of the venue, they pass police cars racing towards the scene of the crime... helicopters are flying overhead shining their light on the parking lot of the venue.

J Loc's heart is still racing as he plops down on the bus' couch with a sigh....

Just then, Strapz begins. "My nigga. You the craziest nigga I eva met in my life, yo! I knew LA niggas wuz wild but Cuz you off the Richter!"

Lover Boy cuts in. "Cuz, you goin' way too hard out here, Loc! We ain't in LA. We ain't at war wit' none of these niggas out here! They just actin' up cuz we in they town shinin' and got they hoes going crazy!"

"Yeah I know Lova Boy, but you know I ain't wit' none of that disrespectful shit 'cuz I'll get active wit' niggaz like it's nothin'!!"

Strapz takes a seat at the tour bus dining table and starts rolling a blunt. As he lights the tip and takes a long pull, he begins to choke while speaking, "I ain't gon' lie, J Loc. Dat wuz tha most gangsta shit I ever saw in my life! Nigga, you jumped from tha stage and went head up with them niggaz! I think you laid a couple niggaz down, G! M Dub Gangsta Crip ain't nothin' to fuck wit!! But you gotta turn it down, my G. I know this shit gonna make the evening news and all fingers will be pointing in our direction. I can see it now: Patrons die at gangster rapper Strapz show in Pittsburg, full story at 11."

J Loc doesn't see the irony of being the initiator of the violence; he's just glad he was the shooter and didn't get shot. Deep down, J Loc knows he made a mistake, but he also knows that once you are in a hole, you have to fight your way out or be left a victim.

Strapz continues, "That ain't good for business, homie. Now hopefully the tour doesn't get shut down once the news hits the wire. But on everything, I ain't even trippin'! Nigga, I'm runnin' wit' tha most gangsta niggaz eva! But just know, tha feds are goin' to be all ova us now so we really got watch it!"

A dead silence comes over the bus momentarily. The

blunt Strapz rolled is making its way around the three of them. J Loc takes a pull and as he passes it back to Strapz he begins to speak. "First off, Cuz, I want to apologize for fuckin' tha show up! I wasn't even trippin' 'til they started flashing they bullshit off brand hood! I guess I just lost it…"

Lover Boy cuts in on the conversation again. "Yeah, but Cuz, you gots to understand this tour is givin' us a way to leave all that shit alone! I ain't fuckin' wit' tha hood from now on, Cuz! I see a way to get it without sellin' dope and goin' to jail and I'm goin' for it! I brought you in, J Loc, because you tha muscle on tha turf, but you also smart, my nigga! You know that shit was fucked up, J Loc, and we can't have that shit. If it happens again, niggas gon' have to send you back home, Cuz!"

J Loc automatically jumps in Lover Boy's face. Lover Boy knows better than to try and discipline J Loc, whether he is wrong or right. J Loc presses his index at Lover Boy's nose. "Cuz I don't know what tha fuck done crawled in yo' ass but you betta calm it down! Wrong or right, I am still callin' shots fo' the hood and you gon' respect protocol, Cuz! If this man don't say I'm leavin', then you ain't got to say shit, Cuz! You been ackin' all weird lately on this rapper shit! Cuz I don't give a fuck about none of that fake shit! Nigga, I'm tha reason you still breathin' in tha hood! You can skate if you want to, but I'm dyin' M Dub, Cuz!"

Strapz has been silently watching the hostility between J Loc and Lover Boy and decides to intervene before it escalates any further. "Yo, Yo! You niggas need to calm down! Y'all both made good points, but I need both of y'all out here! Lover Boy is takin' my stage show up a 100 notches and J Loc, you gonna have the whole world talkin' bout Strapz from what went down at the show. I need both my M Dub niggas, yo!"

J Loc lets out a deep breath. "If it was anybody else but you, Lova Boy, my finga wouldn't have been in they face but in they ass! Cuz, you know that!"

"I know, homie, I just want to make it as a rapper, get out the hood and make my Moms proud! I been a fuck-up my whole life and this is tha only time she has eva told me she was proud of me!"

"I feel that, my nigga! We homies no matter what! M Dubs ova everythang!"

"Gangstas movin' Cuz!"

Strapz jumps back into leadership role. "Now that I got y'all niggas back on my level, J Loc why don't you go online, hit Twitter and Facebook and that shit and tell all the bad bitches we coming to Champaign tomorrow night."

"Fa'sho homie, but I gotta let you know dat once tha hoes see this trey movin', Cuz even you gon' have a hard time gettin' a bitch!"

"Is that right? So you think you gon' get mo' bitches than tha star?"

"Fuckin' right! I always got tha baddest bitches in tha hood! Bitches just love a gangsta nigga! You a rap star, but Cuz, Imma block star!"

"Okay, we gon' see then!"

"Yeah, nigga, you gon' see!"

All three of them start laughing. The tour bus has been fueled up and is headed in route to Champaign.

With the bus hitting a long stretch of the highway, Strapz and Lover Boy have napped out, but J Loc is on the iPad reaching out to females on all levels of social media. While surfing the web, J Loc discovers footage on YouTube of him jumping into a crowd in Pittsburg and unloading his pistol during the altercation. As he sees the footage, he realizes he can no longer can go on stage or be seen with Strapz's entourage until the heat cools off, but that's okay with him. J Loc will be in an even better position to reap the benefits of being on the road. Strapz has put him in charge of Social Media and Internet Marketing. It is now J Loc's job to invite all the bad bitches to the show and get them backstage and if they are lucky, back to the hotel for the afterparty – all via Strapz's Facebook/Twitter/Instagram pages. To J Loc, it's better to stay in the hotel room and get pussy then to be singled out for what went down in Pittsburg – or have it happen again in another city.

Social media sites like Facebook and Twitter are an entirely different situation for a celebrity than it is for most people. Groupies, wannabes, and fans are able to communicate directly with their favorite celebrity in the most intimate of ways. J Loc is amazed at the amount of nude photos that Strapz receives via DM.

Living in Los Angeles, J Loc has been surrounded by the Hollywood star maker machine his entire life but he has never seen it this close up and personal. To a gang leader who survives on intimidation, confrontation, and brutality - the world of entertainment seems like a surreal cartoon. He's not sure he wants any part of it – well, maybe the women part, but that's it. He begins sending messages to the most beautiful women in Champaign to attend the afterparty at the Wimberley Hotel; the most luxurious hotel in town. He reads through at least twenty-five decent prospects but responds to what he considers the top ten beauties. Out of the ten, there are three that he has a definite eye on - Karla, Teresa, and Melanie.

These three dimes will be a good match for him, Strapz, and Lover Boy. He sends all three of the women pictures of him with his shirt off exposing his hood tattoos. He gives the beauties his cell and they begin communicating immediately thru text. The women start sending J Loc naked pictures to ensure they get chosen tonight. J Loc smiles and shows Strapz and Lover Boy the nude pics.

"Nigga, I ain't even no rapper and I got the baddest bitches in tha town... peep!"

A wide-eyed Lover Boy drools over the pictures. "Damn, that bitch is bad, Cuz! But I ain't trippin' tho, I know I'm knockin' down something!! That's on everything!"

Strapz chimes in, "See the difference between us is simple; I don't chase no hoes, they chase me! Groupie love on tha road ain't shit, you ack like you wasn't fuckin' dimes at my crib in Malibu!"

"Yeah, I give you that Strapz! But them Pittsburgh

hoes y'all were fucking with before the show was NOT the business! You put me in charge of the bitches and I handled it, I got two each fo' everybody - don't trip!"

"Yo! Dem bitches you showed us the pictures of was BOMB! Make sure they come through the afterparty and back to tha hotel, homie!"

"I got chu! Truth be told... I'm just fuckin' wit' bitches fo' tha rest of tha tour!"

Laughter erupts from everybody.

J Loc looks down at his phone and sees that Karla has texted him again, he smiles and starts doing his set of push-ups; he has work to put in tonight and wants to be ready.

The tour bus and security pull up to the Wimberley Hotel. Big Bobby, the tour manager and head of security, gets everyone checked in and returns with room keys. As everyone heads for their assigned rooms, J Loc waits an extra twenty minutes on the bus to see if there is any indications that any local or federal agents are there looking for him. When the coast seems clear, he exits the bus and gangsta bails into the hotel.

Strapz and Lover Boy are preparing for tonight's performance and are going back and forth over their routine in their room. Lover Boy is a certified rapper now. He is fully enamored and loving this new life as a performer. For what seems like forever, Lover Boy has been looking for a way out of the violence and mayhem in the streets of Los Angeles; and he has finally found an escape in being on stage with Strapz. J Loc has noticed the change in Lover Boy too. It has always been his job to protect Lover Boy from the more aggressive homies in the neighborhood. And ironically, that's what really defines their friendship. It is like a big brother looking out for a much weaker and smaller brother, but they can both feel that their lives are beginning to head in different directions. J Loc watches as the two rehearse tonight's performance set. When Strapz catches J Loc watching them from a mirror, J Loc throws up Mid City Westside Crip in the air. He doesn't give a fuck about the rap life. He will die a Crip, not a rapper but as a participant in an ongoing war in LA that he is still very much a part of.

J Loc goes to his room to get ready for the girls coming through. They are so excited to meet J Loc that none of them are attending the concert, they are all coming to chill with him at the hotel until the concert is over. Karla texts J Loc to let him know that she and her friends are downstairs in the lobby. J Loc, still leery of any possible law enforcement monitoring of Strapz, tells them to come up to room 1215.

He opens the door and lets them inside his room and is stunned by how gorgeous Karla is in person. She likes what she sees in J Loc, too, and their physical attraction to each other is undeniable.

"Damn girl, I know he fine but show some kind of restraint!" Melanie says loudly and playfully nudges Karla.

"Don't trip, I'm feeling you tha same way Karla! Let me take y'all jackets. Y'all drink, right?" J Loc helps Karla take off her jacket and sees the full shape of her body. He puts both hands over his mouth and lets out a WOW. Karla is a 5'7" redbone with long silky hair that falls down to the middle of her back. The skin-tight dress accents her thick brickhouse frame. With those big titties & a phat ass, J Loc is thinking to himself he's really got a job ahead of him tonight with her. "Ladies let me get you something to drink - you want Muscat, Hennessey, or Moet Rose?"

Teresa looks at J Loc and says, "I'll take some Hennessey, a bitch is tryin' to get faded tonight!"

"That's what's up! What do you want me to get you, Karla?"

Speaking for the first time since she entered the room Karla says, "I will have whatever you want me to have, J."

"Well that's easy, I want you to have me! But before that I'm gonna give you a glass of Hen mixed with Rose. I call it The Turn Up!"

"Well, we gon' have to see if that gets me to Turn Up," Karla says with the sexiest grin and most flirtatious eyes.

J Loc makes everybody's drinks and the mood opens up even more as all four sip their drinks.

Teresa, the most ratchet of the three, starts the conversation. "So J Loc, you know you the first real Crip we have met in Champaign. Everybody out here is either People or Folk!"

"Is that right? I can't believe it ain't been no real Rip ridaz out this bitch!"

"It has been some fake ass Crips from Down South up here frontin' with they country asses! Wasn't nobody feelin' them niggas!"

"Yeah, it be a lot of off-brand shit goin' on in these areas, but y'all dealin' wit' a real one from the town right here!"

Melanie, arguably just as gorgeous as Karla, is the obvious choice to hook up with Strapz, seems to also be feeling J Loc. "Girl, he talk so funny! Your lil accent is cute though! J Loc, you is probably the cutest gangsta I seen in years! You got that thick wavy hair and them light brown eyes!"

Teresa quickly checks Melanie. "Ughh! Girl, why you sayin' all that? You know Karla all on that boy!"

"Shit! Bitch, I'm just callin' it likes I see it!"

J Loc moves closer to Karla on the couch. "She ain't trippin'! Karla know she got all my attention! Y'all supposed to be fuckin' wit' tha homies after the show anyway! By tha time them niggas get here y'all gon' be good and drunk and ready fo' my niggas!"

"I guess! We real bitches tho! Most of these rap niggas is fake or either gay! Yo' niggas ain't gay is they, J Loc?"

"Ay Karla, you might wanna get yo' girl - she way outta bounds on that stupid shit!"

J Loc laughs. "Hell naw! Them niggas ain't gay or fake! My nigga Strapz really wit' tha biz!!"

"Okay, I'm just sayin'! I like gangsta dick! I don't

want no bullshit!"

"Check this out lil mama, I'm certified, and my niggas is too!" J Loc grins widely.

J Loc and the three gorgeous females are having a great time, laughing, telling stories, and drinking. They were enjoying themselves so much, they all lost track of time – until Strapz and Lover Boy bust into the room.

"YO! Tonight's show was off the hook, my nigga!!! I wish you was there J Loc! This was probably the best show yet!"

"Whoa... whoa... whoa... what do we have here?" says Lover Boy, checking out the three lovely ladies.

"J Loc, you in here gettin' it poppin, huh? Who are these pretty ladies... introduce yo' boy!" Strapz exclaims.

"Nah, nah we were just chillin' until y'all got here. Ladies, let me introduce y'all – Strapz, Lover Boy – meet Teresa and Melanie."

They all exchange hellos, how ya doin's hugs and hand shakes. But Strapz notices one introduction was left out. "Yo, J Loc, who is the bad one over there you didn't introduce to us, homie? I wanna meet her..."

"Fall back homie – this is Karla. I'm already callin' dibs, G, so fall back."

"My bad Loc, my bad... Do ya thang!"

Strapz and Lover Boy immediate begin to cozy up with Teresa and Melanie, who begin pouring more drinks while Strapz rolls up a blunt.

"Ladies, I hope y'all ain't on the bougie shit, because

we about to turn this party up."

"Bougie? Nigga please! Hurry up and roll that weed up – I'm ready to get high!"

With all the laughter and chuckling going on, J Loc and Karla make their way to the back bedroom. Once there, J Loc closes the door and guides Karla to the bed. J Loc begins kissing and touching all over Karla. She doesn't resist, they both know what they are there for and the time has come. J Loc takes his shirt off, showcasing his thugged out physique. Karla admires him with a big smile and runs her hands over the tattoos on his chest. J Loc in his most serious, gangster tone asks Karla, "You ready for the Loc, baby?"

"You know I am."

7

Cargo Heisting

Damu and Brazyiak plan to pull off a $5 million dollar cargo heist of stolen goods from the Los Angeles Harbor Gateway with the help of the Eastside Laotian Bloods and the Korean Bloods. Damu has brokered a deal to commandeer a cargo barge full of clothes, shoes, and electronics. The Laotian Bloods in the projects on the eastside put him on to it through their Asian Uno card. That's the Prison program that all the Asians unify under while in jail. They respect the "B" fully, plus this is a good way to gain their trust and further solidify the Blood movement in jail and on the streets. This heist furthers Damu's plan for a unified Blood Alliance in Los Angeles by strengthening the ties of trust between the Black Blood sets and Asian Bloods sets, but most importantly, the heist nets him and Brazyiak a cool million dollars in profit to be split evenly amongst the two.

The plan is to grab the cargo barge, attach it to an 18-wheeler and bring it to the Korean Bloods off of Western Avenue and 3rd Street. They in turn will distribute the goods throughout the southland through their network of family owned retail stores and swap meets.

Damu and Brazyiak are driving down the 110 southbound. At its farthest end southbound, The Harbor Gateway freeway ends at the "Ports of Call" where all of Los Angeles' import and export business is conducted.

They are about twenty minutes out from the port. "Okay, Brazyiak, Blood, let's run over the program one more time before we touch down!"

"Blood, is you sure this shit is gonna work? Because if not, I'm smokin' security on sight... on bloods!"

"Yeah, I'm sure. Now let's go over the plan. You pull up in the cab of the truck. What do you say to the Security Guard at the gate?"

"I pull up and ask for the bay number, then give him this paperwork, and wait for him to show me which bay to park the truck at."

"Good, you got it Blood, then what?"

"Then I drive this big motherfucker to the bay, give my paperwork to the bay manager, wait 'til he directs me to the bay with the work. Imma back the truck cab in and attach it to the cargo trailer, then I'm up out of there."

"Just like you suppose to be! You got it, my G. Now where's the fake license I gave you earlier?"

"Right here, Blood, in the shirt pocket of this slim ass work shirt you got me! And don't ask on the gloves, homie, you see I got these brownies on!"

"And underneath the gloves, what do you have?"

Brazyiak is frustrated with all the questions Damu is asking. Letting out a sigh, he responds, "Surgicals, homie.

C'mon Blood, I been killin' Crabs and murkin' niggas for years, homie, and ain't never went down. You know the business on mine, I'm official with this shit!"

"Right, but I have murders on these fingerprints, homie, and you know if I get caught, I'm finito, over, them crackas gon' give a nigga 100 years! The Blood Alliance needs me to pull this one through so I'm just making sure we straight on everythang!"

"Nigga, don't trip, the hood needs you, big homie, we gon' be good money!"

Damu pulls up to the empty truck cab parked on 12th and Gaffey Street. Brazyiak hops out with a focused look in his eye, ready for the heist.

"Once you grab the cargo, meet me at the underpass of the 110/105 interchange – Imma follow you to K-Town from there."

Brazyiak responds, "Whoop."

The mission is about to go down.

Brazyiak jumps in the empty cab, starts the engine, and drives towards the loading dock main gate. The security guard at the gate asks for Brazyiak's ID. Brazyiak gives the man the info with one hand and keeps the other hand on his lap close to his gun in case anything funny happens, then he is ready to attack.

"Everything looks okay to me. Just take a right and continue until you see the bay number you are looking for, sir."

Brazyiak smiles back at the security guard and says,

"Thank you, good sir!"

The security guard has no idea that the wrong answer on his part would have cost him his life. Brazyiak drives the 18-wheeler over to the bay give their forged paperwork to the dock manager. After review, he tells Brazyiak to back his cab into the trailer. Three longshoreman assist in hooking the trailer up to the cab.

Damu is on the freeway headed south to the 110/105 interchange where he will meet Brazyiak. While driving, he calls the Korean connection in K Town to let them know their estimated time of arrival with the goods. "Soo Whoop, K Dog! This is Damu. We are loading the truck up now and should be on Olympic at the location in about two hours. I will call you again when we are en route."

Back at the loading dock, Brazyiak stands at the back of the truck watching every move the workers make while hitching the truck up. He does not trust anyone and is always looking for any opportunity to let out his anger. But the workers stay diligently on their job, unbeknownst to his wrath.

The whole operation is complete at just under 1 hour. Brazyiak jumps into the truck, and chunks the deuce to the docks' security guards as they usher him out with over one million dollars of stolen merchandise.

Once out of their view, Brazyiak starts bouncing with excitement in the driver's seat. He calls Damu and says, "Damu I got in and outta there real quick, bro! We finna get some serious bands off this play for real though!"

Damu is already posted at the interchange, sitting low in the leather seats of his BMW. He answers Brazyiak with a "Whoop…"

"Imma be there in ten minutes, Blood."

Damu hangs up and falls into deep thought while cars whisk thru the interchange. He is looking at how this criminal act has come to fruition as a bonding element between the Asian Bloods and the Blood Alliance. He thinks to hisself, "This is a very good beginning with us and the Asian Bloods. They are able to see that we handle business and keep our word. We are moving the Blood Alliance in the right direction!"

At that moment, Brazyiak is driving thru the interchange blowing the horn of the 18-wheeler. Damu lets his seat up, starts his engine, and flicks his lights twice to Brazyiak to let him know he's right behind him.

It is early morning in Los Angeles and traffic is the lightest it will be all day on the 101 freeway. Brazyiak brings the truck to the Olympic exit downtown, makes a left and drives into K-Town.

K-Town, or Korea Town, is LA's fastest growing urban neighborhood. In the 20 years since the riots, this part of the city has exploded as the place to live between Hollywood and downtown Los Angeles. The area is home to many afterhours clubs and lounges and bustles at this time with party revelers. Brazyiak parks the truck behind a nondescript minimall plaza on Olympic next to an all-night pool hall. Damu parks his BMW right in front of the truck and jumps out. A slight Korean youth with a red baseball hat and red shirt walks to the front of the truck and throws up the "B" hand sign. It is "K Dog" the Korean connection.

"Soo whoop! Damu, it's me, K Dog! Good to see y'all made it with no problems."

Damu exchanges the Blood handshake with K Dog, but K Dog is focused on the gangster stance and posture of Brazyiak who has just exited the driver's side of the truck and yells, "What up wit' it, K Dog? Let's get to this fuckin' money on Dub S GB!"

K Dog can not believe he is meeting WSGB living legend Brazyiak and the father indirectly of his hood. He feels he has to tell Brazyiak their association. "I gotcha, homie!! You know we named our hood after the Dub S GB, right? The big homies was fucking with Big Flame from your hood!"

Brazyiak moves in swiftly in on K Dog and they are now face to face. "Yeah, I know the biz. I brought the big homie over here from the eastside. He told me before he got smoked about y'all! I keep my eye on anything with the Dub S on it. But y'all gonna have to check in with me if it move under the name you got or it's gon' be problems!"

Damu quickly steps in to intervene as usual right before things escalate to violence with Brazyiak. "Brazyiak, you can handle that issue at another time. We all have more pressing matters to take care of between all of us."

Brazyiak doesn't flinch. He stares K Dog down while telling Damu, "Yeah, I got chu. But we gonna work this situation out though K Dog!"

K Dog doesn't move either. He stares back at Brazyiak and says, "I got that, homie."

The two slowly separate and stand on both sides of Damu.

"K Dog, the homies on the eastside speak very highly of you and this operation was done as a gesture of faith and for all of us to make money but most importantly to connect us through our shared lineage and have your hood join the Blood Alliance."

"No doubt, we respect what you doing out here for the card. It is about time that all the dogs get back together again!"

Damu nods his head in agreement and says, "I was told that your family owns the majority of the swap meets in the city and will be able to get rid of all the electronics without detection."

"Yeah that's right. And we will buy the whole shipment for two million. A million for you and Brazyiak, and a million for the eastside homies."

"That's exactly what I was told. Do you have the cash on you or are we going somewhere else to get it?"

"No, I have the money nearby. Let me go in the pool hall and I will be right back."

K Dog sprints inside the pool hall to get the cash. Damu and Brazyiak do not say a word to each other, as they stand on the street waiting for K Dog, their shadows are illuminated from the neon signs that light up the mini mall plaza. They don't know if K Dog is coming back out with the money or with an aggressive move based on how Brazyiak approached him earlier. They are preparing for anything to happen. Good or bad.

K Dog walks out with a large duffle bag and hands it to Damu for inspection. "It is all there, big homie, for you to count."

Damu opens the bag and says, "I will make the official count in a few hours. If there are any discrepancies I will contact you directly, K Dog. Welcome to the family!"

"Thank you Damu, we are happy to get down with you and move with the best in the Bity."

"You are in with us now. Aye, can you guys to do me a favor and dump the truck by the 10 freeway on Vermont? Some people will be looking for it there."

"Done deal, Damu." K Dog steps back towards the shadows.

Brazyiak looks inside the bag and smiles with a devilish grin. "And to think that I was gon' shoot K Dog and he had all this money waiting for us!" They both laugh as they hop into Damu's Beamer.

As they head towards Ladera Heights, their discussion revolves around their cut from the heist and how they will launder it. The plan is to split $500k between each other now, and put the other $500k into an offshore account through the Armenians. Damu suggests, "Let's head up to Hollywood tonight and holla at Kamir at Club Apex"

"Apex? Hell naw!! Nigga, I wanna hit that

underground strip party they be havin' in Hollywood called Discrete ,tho! That shit is turnt up all the way I heard!"

"Brazyiak, we are not just going to party. We are going out to get our money laundered. It just so happens the club is where they handle they business."

Damu and Brazyiak move thru the back streets of K Town heading south bound.

———————————————————

Later that night, they are getting prepared for a night out at the Apex club. The freshest outfits are laid out, cologne is being sprayed, and music is playing loudly in the background. Damu and Brazyiak are in a celebratory vibe. And why shouldn't they be? They just earned $500,000 each for a few hours work. This is their time to shine and these two can do it amongst the best of them in Hollywood.

Brazyiak flexes in his bathroom mirror and yells out to Damu, "Damu, I don't think these hoes is gonna be ready for a Dub SG tonight! I'm way too saucy with this Ferragamo and En Noir fit on 'em!! And this new Tom Ford is brazy blood! Come smell it!"

Damu walks in front of Brazyiak's room and answers him in the doorway, "The new Tom Ford smells bomb. What car do you want to take?"

"Come on, homie! We need the Bent out there chuuchin' for us. The feet and the paint murder blacked out is that feeling for tonight! I'm on some Flying Spur shit!"

"Yeah the Flying Spur feels good for tonight. Let's do that, but hurry up, pretty boy! You take too long in the mirror!"

"Ain't that a bitch! Nigga look just like me and he calling me pretty boy! Fuck you homie! I'll be ready in ten."

Soon after the two are dressed, they are smashing the Bentley down La Cienega, headed up to Hollywood . While Damu swoops lane to lane though traffic, Brazyiak is hanging out of the window and hollering at any attractive woman they pass by on the streets. Their present mood is jovial and carefree for the moment. They both know that they will probably have way more fun now than they will in the club. It's easy to pull a bitch in LA when you in a ride like this. Plus, when they reach Club Apex, it will be all business, no games, as they focus on the business they are doing with the Armenian gangsters. A lot of money is at stake.

They pull into the line for valet and it is spilling out onto the Cahuenga corridor. The parking lot looks like an exotic car photo shoot. There are Lambos, Ferraris, Rolls Royces, Buggatis, and any other foreign car that is over $100,000 parked there. Damu and Brazyiak exit the Bentley and head to the VIP entrance. It is a madhouse of energy. There are athletes, rappers, actors, and groupies all clamoring to get in. Damu has been given a code word to tell the main security guard. Brazyiak is holding on to the duffle with the money in it. They make their way to the front, tell the main bouncer the word, and another security guard comes and walks them to another side of the building. He knocks on the brick wall of the building and a secret entrance opens. They follow him down a short hallway and land in a gigantic room filled with Armenian gangsters and beautiful women of every ethnicity. Drinks are flowing, hookahs are being smoked, mollys are being popped, and cocaine is being sniffed. This is truly a den of iniquities. Damu surveys the room and looks for his connect Kamir. He sees him in a corner smoking a Cuban cigar.

"As salaam alaikum, Brother Kamir!"

Kamir stands up and hugs Damu. "Walaikum Salaam, Brother Damu. I see you made it here in health and good spirits."

"As always. Inshaallah, that it continues like that. How is your brother Samir?"

"Samir is Samir. He is locked up in Pelican Bay right now. He asked about you in his last letter to me."

Samir and Damu were locked up in YA together and became good friends through bonding in Islam. Samir and Kamir are the sons of the biggest Lebanese-Armenian mobster in Los Angeles and have free reign of any criminal activity in that world.

"Tell Samir I said greetings, but you know what I am here for good brother."

"Of course I do. Let me get my father's business partner with the club and have him get started on everything. I'll be right back!"

Damu takes a seat where Kamir was. Brazyiak has been standing the whole time and enjoying the debauchery that is going on around him. He catches the eye of one of the gorgeous pieces of eye candy that the Armenian mobsters have. He likes what he sees and so does she. Holding the duffle bag at his waist, he just has to say something to her.

"Damn! Baby, you fine as hell! What's yo' name?"

The woman smiles at Brazyiak, but before she can say a word her Armenian date grabs her arm and pushes her out of the view of Brazyiak before he speaks. "What the fuck are you doing back here, nigger? This is only for our people!"

Brazyiak drops the duffle bag and immediately lays a barrage of blows to the man's head and he falls quickly. Within seconds, guns are drawn by the Armenian mobsters and they surround Brazyiak. He dares them to shoot him.

"If you gon' shoot me, then do it Blood! ON WSGB do it, muthafuckas!"

Damu races across the room. He only has a few moments to react or Brazyiak will be murdered right here in Club Apex.

"Whoa! Listen! I am Kamir's friend. We are here as his invited guests handling business! Let's all calm down and take a breather. He is coming back in here with one of the co-owners. Let's not make any rash decisions, fellas!"

As if on cue, Kamir and his father's business partner walk in the room and see the hostile situation and go into diffusement mode.

"Brother Damu! What is going on?"

"Kamir I think some of your guys approached my brother Brazyiak in an inappropriate manner and things escalated from there. I am just trying to get calmer heads to prevail."

The mobsters talk in their native language to Kamir. Even though you can't understand their vernacular, the exchange is definitely hostile. The guns are put away and the guy who called Brazyiak a nigger apologizes. Everyone in the room realizes that to confront Kamir is to confront his father and no one wants those type of problems.

As everyone moves back to their seats, Kamir, Damu, Brazyiak and his father's business partner move into the corner and discuss the business at hand. Introductions are in order.

"My name is Dave and I am Kamir's father's right hand man. We both own the club together. I apologize for any disrespect to you and your brother!"

Damu shakes Dave's hand. "No problem. In the life that we lead we expect anything to happen. The way you resolved the problem shows the honor and dignity of your character. Now what I would like to do at this time, Dave and Kamir, is get this business taken care of."

"By all means, Damu. Let me explain to you how everything works. We will have two offshore accounts in your name in Russia and Lebanon. It will take five days for the transfers to take place and then you are able to do what you want to with them. Our operational fee is $20,000 and we will be depositing $480,000, correct?"

"Correct," Damu says as Brazyiak to hands Dave the duffle bag. Dave looks inside to see the money.

Damu looks him in his eyes. "As a man of honor, Dave,

I take your word on everything you say but I do want you to know that if anything occurs outside of the parameters of our deal then there will be severe repercussions that you will have to deal with!"

"I understand that and I stand behind everything that I have said. Now as a sign of good business between you and I, my friend, you must take shots of the best Russian vodka that money can buy!" Dave motions a waitress who brings over a bottle and pours four shot glasses for the gentlemen.

"Let's make a toast," Dave says. "To Damu, a man of integrity and intelligence!" They all four take the shots.

Brazyiak, already feeling good from the shot says, "Damu, I'm headed over to the VIP area in the club where the bitches are! I'm tired of being around these garlic eating muthafuckas, homie! I need to let loose!"

"Come on then G, I think we deserve a good time!"

8

Damu's Reflection

After a night of revelry and almost getting killed in Hollywood trying to launder the illegal money from the Koreans, Damu stops by Echo Park to reminisce on his mother and the life they shared before he moved into the Jungles and became a Blood.

Man, last night was wilder than a motherfucker!!

It's 6:30am in this beautiful city of Los Angeles. The smog has been lifted, the sun is out, but the city is still asleep. I usually get up about an hour before this and make my early morning salat. That prayer is the most powerful prayer of the day because you are waking up very early, proving your dedication to Allah. It always clears my head up after I pray; then I meditate in silence for about twenty minutes to organize my thoughts for the day. After the whole process, I am refueled and re-energized to face my upcoming day.

This morning as I drive from the nightclub in Hollywood down Sunset, with the warm rising sun beaming on my back, I start to fall into my early morning self-reflection mode. I would normally take La Brea back home to Ladera Heights, but I decide to continue eastbound down Sunset.

It's an odd reflective vibe that I'm feeling this morning, something from my past is telling me to head eastward and I instinctively follow it. My mom and I used to get up early and walk and exercise around this time.

As I drive eastward past East Hollywood and into Silverlake, emotions and memories start to overcome me. My mom would wake up early to exercise as part of her rehab regiment. She learned how to work out as a way to release endorphins to combat her cravings for heroin and methadone. It's crazy how I had put thoughts of my mom deep in the back of my mind and out of my daily thoughts. It's a coping mechanism I guess, something I developed as a child to help me deal with the loss of the greatest love of my life, but as I travel down Sunset Boulevard my feelings and my tears are starting to flow. The homie Brazyiak is sleeping in my passenger seat, but even if he was not, I would not stop crying.

The tears falling are for my dead homie, my first homie, my mom.

As I drive from Silverlake to Echo Park, the emotions really hit me because I used to come visit my aunt here with my mom. I have a lot of good memories over here from my youth. We would walk to Pioneer Chicken on Echo Park Avenue and mom would always order an Orange Bang for me and a horchata for herself, but my favorite thing over here is right where I am pulling up... the park – Echo Park.

I used to love walking around the lake at Echo Park with Mom.

We would get up early at around 5:30am and drive over from East Los to the lake and start walking making our way around it by 6:15am. Mom and I would talk about everything as we walked the park and around the Lake. No subject was off limits. The more we walked, the more we talked about my school days, my friends, and about how Mom was dealing with her sobriety issues, but the conversations I enjoyed the most with her were about my family history in Mexico and Los Angeles.

Mom would tell me how our family came from Durango four generations ago to East Los Angeles and started one of the oldest grocery chains on the eastside. She would speak on how she met my father when she was a Brown Beret and he was a spokesperson for the Black Power Young Bloods at a Community Gang Intervention Summit in East St. Louis when she was a teenager. She would tell me how she loved my dad from the first moment she laid eyes on him. It took almost ten years for them to evolve as a couple, of which I become a product of. Those conversations are some of the strongest memories I have of my mom, so this lake is like a sacred place to me. As I wipe these falling tears from my face and look around me I realize now that I have to change a lot of things in my life.

My mother's death affected me so severely that the only way for me to go forward was to let go of every memory that I ever had of her. I did not want to deal with anything that reminded me of her. Not her family, not East Los Angeles, nothing!! Shit, I don't even like eating Mexican food anymore because it brings up memories of my mom in the kitchen cooking meals for me. But now is the time to reconcile with the memories of my mother and the man that I am. I need to honor and cherish those fleeting moments I had with my life nurturer and embrace all her love that she provided me with. If I'm trying to lead the Bloods into a new light, then I need to lead by example and pull myself out of the dark shadowy hole of my Mom's death. She is gone, but never forgotten. I will love you always, Mommy.

And now I need to clear my head this early morning and what better way than getting out of this car and walking around the Lake in the park like mom and I used to do.

Allah Hu Akbar.

I have work to do now... and it's time to start. NOW.

9

Big Trouble in Milwaukee

Strapz's tour bus pulls into its last stop in Milwaukee. The shows have been dope, even with the drama that ensued in Pittsburg; Strapz has recharged his battery and is ready to get back to Malibu and record new music. Lover Boy has decided that he is going to quit gangbanging and continue pursuing music with Strapz. J Loc has just had an incredible time in the previous town with a beautiful woman named Karla. J Loc believes she's a keeper and plans on sending her out to LA to visit him once things become less hectic in his life. Everyone is in a good mood and ready to wrap the tour up and head back to Los Angeles.

At the Orion Hotel, the entourage exits the bus and heads inside. There is boisterous conversation amongst the crew about the exploits the last few nights. Just then, the local concert promoters greet Strapz in the lobby.

"My man, Gangsta D! What's good wit' it, Cuz?"

"Strapz my nigga! Glad you made to the Milltown safe! Man, I saw what happened out there in Pittsburgh, I hope we don't have no problems like that here tonight!"

"Naw, naw, we all good Gangsta D. That didn't

really have nothing to do with us anyway, that was the local knuckleheads in there trippin', we good tho'."

Gangsta D nods. Standing in the middle of a circle flanked by five gigantic Gangster Disciples and his teenage son, Lil Gangsta D, Big Gangsta D motions to one of his massive henchmen to step forward and he hands a brown paper bags to Strapz.

"The whole one hunnit racks is right there, Strapz! You might want to go upstairs and count that!"

"Done deal... Ay yo! J Loc, Lover Boy, let's go to the room and handle this business."

J Loc hears Strapz's orders and cuts right through the circle of Gangsta Disciples to get to Strapz and head towards the elevator. When he does this, J Loc walks in a way to assert his position on the gangster food chain.

Just then, Lil Gangsta D proclaims, "Oh shit! On Hoover! You tha nigga on the news they say shot them niggas in Pittsburgh! This nigga G right here, Pops!" Lil Gangsta D breaks through the circle to shake J Loc's hand and says, "You know in tha feds, GDs and Crips is like cuzzins!"

"Fa'sho, my niggas locked up told me when we cool wit' y'all. It's called the eight-ball! I'm already knowin'!"

"Pops, I want to stay here in the hotel wit' Strapz and J Loc fo' a minute. Send somebody to come and get me befo' tha show!"

"Aight. Strapz, now you take care of my boy. And scrap the afterparty; the venue pulled out because of the shit that jumped off in Pittsburgh, they said they didn't want to bring the gangs out. So after tha show, we need you to do a couple verses for the artists on my label!"

"Shit, that shouldn't be a problem. The only thing I see that's gon' be a problem is countin' all this cash! Next time Cuz, we gon' do a bank deposit or wire transfer or something!"

"I give it out like I get it! I'll see y'all later on tonight afta tha show!"

Gangsta D and his guys leave the hotel as Strapz, J Loc, Lover Boy, and Lil Gangsta D head to the room.

Upstairs in Strapz's room, J Loc starts the arduous task of counting one hundred thousand dollars' worth of cash by hand. He empties all the money on one of the beds, lights a blunt, pours a cup of Hennessey, and goes to work stacking the bills in piles of one thousand.

Lil Gangsta D asks J Loc if he can hit the blunt. J Loc silently passes it over to him as he continues counting stacks.

Taking two pulls, it's obvious Lil Gangsta D is an amateur. Cough, cough. "Damn! That must be dat Cali Kush right there!"

"That's all niggas smoke, Cuz!"

"Yeah, I fucks wit' a lot of Crip niggas out here. What set you from?"

"Nigga, the only set that mattas. Mid City Westside Gangsta Crips, Cuz!"

"Yeah I heard of y'all. I fucked heavy wit' some Eastside Gangsta Crips!"

"Yeah, them tha big homies on the east. But shiittt, you betta watch out fuckin' wit' them eastsidas tho, Cuz!"

"I ain't trippin' on no niggas! I'm Lil Gangsta D! My Pops got it sewed up from Milwaukee to Chicago! Tha worst thang a nigga can do is fuck wit' me!"

J Loc hears Lil Gangsta D, but is still concentrating on counting the money. Words mean very little to J Loc. He lives in the world where actions speak louder than words, and anyone at any time can get it.

Later that night...

Strapz and the entourage are boarding the tour bus to get to the venue. J Loc stays behind to finish counting the show money in Strapz's room. He and Lil Gangsta D have been talking and smoking blunts the entire time. The Cali Kush has Lil Gangsta D high as a muthafucka – nodding in and out of consciousness.

On the bus, Strapz receives a phone call from his agent back in Los Angeles. "Goldstein! What's happenin' wit' it?"

"Strapz, you are not going to believe this, man! I just got a call from Quentin Tarantino's office, he wants you in his new movie! He has been seeing you all over the news because of that Pittsburgh shooting incident and says you will bring just the right amount of realism to this role he has in mind for you. I need you to get on the first thing smoking tonight because we have a meeting at 10am tomorrow!"

"It's nothin'! I'll jump a flight after tha show straight

into Van Nuys."

"Sounds good Strapz. I'll send a car to come get you at the airport."

Strapz cannot believe how the coverage of the J Loc shooting incident has led to him getting a part in a major movie. It finally seems like he is about to hit the big time.

At the venue, Gangsta D and a caravan of four black Suburban trucks meet them. Gangsta D and some of his men jump out and onto the tour bus.

"Gangsta D, you just tha man I need to see! Look, there's been a slight change of plans. I need to fly outta here right afta tha show and head back to LA for a meeting. As soon as I finish my biz out there, I'll slide back out here on my own dime tomorrow night and do whateva you need me to do for yo' artists son!"

Gangsta D shakes his head in disappointment. He can't believe what he is hearing come out of Strapz's mouth. "On Hoova! Strapz, we gon' have a problem wit' that move, chalee!"

"What you mean a problem, Cuz? I told you as soon as I finished everything up in LA that I would pay for my flight back out here tomorrow night and do whateva you need! How tha fuck is that a problem, yo? I ain't stiffin' you on shit! I just gotta handle somethin' real quick!"

"On GD, shit don't look or feel right! As the main shotcaller out here, I can't be lettin' niggas tell me what they gon' do and what they ain't gon' do! I gotta power struggle out here wit' deese Milltown niggas already! Wit' me bein' from da Chi, dey always lookin' at ways dat dey can move in on me! If word got out on tha street that I let a rapper push me around or change my plans, then niggas gon' come at me!"

"My nigga, you ain't changin' shit, I'll be back tomorrow. Who tha fuck is gon' know?"

"Niggas in my squad, that's who! The artists you gon' record wit' is from up here, it will spread in the whole city by tha time you get back. Niggaz is all set-up for it to go down tonight. I'm sorry, Strapz, but I can't let you get on that plane until you record dem songs fo' me!"

"Then we both got a problem, homie, 'cuz I ain't turnin' down a meetin' wit' Quentin Tarantino to record a couple songs wit' some nobodies from out here!"

"Then I guess we all just fucked up then, gangsta!"

Gangsta D motions for his team to block the tour bus door from outside, while his GDs inside the bus pull out their guns. At that same moment, Strapz's security pulls out their weapons.

"Gangsta D, what we gonna do, Cuz? I gotta be inside to start the show in thirty ... now we can handle this like grown men, or we can get into some gangsta shit!"

The tension is so thick you can taste it... Any sudden moves and things can get ugly very quick.

Gangsta D doesn't say a word. He stares at Strapz with his killers on standby.

Strapz knows that in all likelihood there is going to be some form of gun-play if he doesn't figure out an option and fast. All he wants to do is defuse this situation so he can make it back to LA for his meeting with Tarantino. Lover Boy is standing behind Strapz texting J Loc. He's giving him the play by play on what's been going on. Lover Boy has always looked at J Loc as the big brother that he never had and that J Loc would be there to help him with threats of violence. It is the nature of their relationship. And right now they need J Loc fast!

"Look Gangsta D, I told you I'll be back to following day... I know we ain't about to do this over no funky ass rap verses, are we?'

Gangsta D does not blink or take his gaze from Strapz. "Fuck that, I done already paid you, Strapz. I'm not finna to be chasin' no punk ass rapper around the globe for no verse! You here tonight. Let's get it done tonight. Now it's simple as that."

"Fuck that shit, Gangsta D! Lemme smoke this fool!" shouts one of his soldiers.

J Loc reads these frantic texts back at the hotel. Lil Gangsta D is passed out from smoking that potent Cali Kush. J Loc laughs out loud and thinks to himself how phony rappers are. At every confrontation with a real threat from the streets, Strapz has had to use J Loc to rescue him. To him, it just reinforces how his lifestyle back in Los Angeles with all of its murder, treachery, and mayhem has prepared him for survival and an innate ability to fight back no matter the odds.

J Loc grabs all the sheets off the bed and uses them

as restraints, wrapping them around Lil Gangsta D while he is incoherent in his chair. He pulls out his iPhone and takes a picture of Lil Gangtsa D tied up, then he cocks back his right arm back and punches Lil Gangsta D so hard that he wakes him up from his weed stupor and knocks him still tied in the chair to the floor.

"Gotdamn, gangsta! What da fuck is wrong wit' you, J Loc? Why you hit me? Why I am I tied up?"

J Loc takes another picture of Lil Gangsta D, this time of him lying on the floor tied up.

"Cuz, your Pops is trippin! It ain't nothin' personal, just bizness!"

"Nigga! You don't know who you fuckin' with! My daddy is gon' kill yo' niggaz!"

"Oh yeah? Well, then Imma kill you."

J Loc sends the pictures to Lover Boy.

Lover Boy looks at the pictures of Lil Gangsta D tied up and can't believe it. He hands the phone over to Strapz and shows him the pictures. Strapz smiles and hands the phone over to Gangsta D.

"I think you might wanna see this, Gangsta D."

"What the fuck you givin' me the phone fo', nigga?" Gangsta D sees the pictures and throws the phone down. "You muthafuckas just signed y'all death certificates! You Crabs is dead!"

Strapz picks up the phone and calls J Loc. "Gangsta D, my man wants to speak to you."

Gangsta D snatches the phone from Strapz hand.

"Look nigga! If you touch my son..."

J Loc cuts him off. "Cuz, jus' chill out wit' all that tough talk! I got yo' son tied up and I will blow his muthafuckin' head off if you don't let my niggas outta there! Ain't no negotiatin' on nothin'! It's yo' son for my niggas!"

Gangsta D hands the phone back to Strapz without a word being said. If he thought letting Strapz leaving town without recording was a problem, he knows once word gets out that his son has been beaten up and kidnapped, every gangster in Milwaukee will be at his head. He has to suppress this information with the quickness. He motions for the soldiers outside and tells his folks on the bus to stand down. As he leaves the bus, he turns to Strapz and says, "Youse a cold nigga, Strapz! Don't eva come back to Milwaukee or Chicago or I will kill you... MY WORD!"

The situation handled, J Loc unties and walks Lil Gangsta D into the lobby of the hotel where he is met by Gangsta D's soldiers. He hands him over to them and walks outside to a cab waiting to take him to meet the tour bus. He shuffles with the Crip gangsta stroll on his exit out the lobby and throws the Mid City Westside Gangsta Crip sign in the air before entering the cab.

10

SOFITEL MACKIN'

CHT realizes that his dream of becoming a top-rated pimp is becoming a reality as he changes his operation from the shitty motel tracks on Century Boulevard to the Sofitel in Beverly Hills. Since the addition of Anna, a nineteen-year-old waif thin but busty, natural blonde Polish bitch to his stable, CHT has elevated his pimp game. With only two white bitches, CHT is making thousands of dollars a day and entering into the Hollywood power circles through his clientele. He is almost where he wants to be as a rising, successful pimp.

Victory. Dominance. Winning. Champion. These words are running through CHT's head as he looks out on Beverly Hills from the balcony of his suite at the Sofitel. Life is good as he's smoking a paper plane of the best medical marijuana and drinking Louie the XVI from a snifter bought from Tiffany's.

While taking pulls off his tightly rolled joint, CHT begins to think on how this all came to be. Damn, I finally have the operation up and running that I have been seeing in my head for a while now. I gotta thank the Pimp God for putting Suga in my path and allowing him to tighten the laces on my pimp shoes. I went from burnt-out motels on Century Boulevard to corporate tricks in the Hollywood Hills, spendin' thousands a day.

Now it really started rollin' once I cracked Anna at the Beverly Center Fashion Mall. I mean, come on! A 5'10" blonde, blue-eyed, big-tittied Polish bitch came up to me smilin' and sayin' hello; shiiit... I had to mack that! She was fresh off the plane from Poland and I knocked her Day One in the town. She said she spoke to me because she thought I was Kobe Bryant! I told her that in this game, I don't dribble, I breaks hoes 'til they cripple! Ya feel me? Her English wasn't that good and I do not speak a word of Polish, but we were both feelin' each other. It was all that magnetic pimp game just drawing her in. I took her to the Sofitel in Beverly Hills that night and got that pussy so wet and didn't even touch it. Just my charisma and savoir-faire was enough. She couldn't believe it; she thought I was about to Mandingo that pussy! I told her straight like this, in order to please me, you gots to cheese me! I let her know my love was different from any other man she had ever met in her life. I told her I needed her to show me she cared for me by giving me money.

I pulled out about ten bands in twenties and I told her that anything she wanted from me I would buy for her and all she had to do was ask. I told her that I was true to those I loved and I expected her to be the same way with me. My game was so thick that the bitch started crying. She opened up like a clam about how her stepdad had stuck his finger up her pussy when she was young and had continued to fuck her ever since. She had been turnin' tricks for free for years.

I brought the game and regulation to the bitch and just like any renegade bitch that is blessed with the knowledge of what a hoe is supposed to do, she instantly fell in love with this pimpin'. From that point on it was all about maximizing my assets off Anna's pussy. You see, Cindy was cool, she was pretty, young, and shaped like a black bitch, but rich white tricks don't want a white bitch shaped like a black bitch, they want them titties! These corporate CEOs want that artificial cold European look and I had a bitch with that look in the stable. Anna knew that I wanted her to sell that pussy, but she knew that I wanted her to do it in the most upscale and luxurious way possible. We stayed in the hotel another two nights before the idea hit me on how to use my new bitch to the max.

CHT was gonna put her on the professional athletes he knew. Almost all the niggas he played with at LMU who had gone pro were full-time ballin' in the cash money now. One of his tightest partners from school, Todd Williams, had just got traded to the LA Clippers from the Orlando Magic. He could also become his biggest trick; if CHT could get Anna on him he would tell all the other players in the league, which in turn would put me in that exclusive Hollywood Hills clientele. CHT got on the iPad and hit him up via Twitter. I sent him a direct message with my phone number and told him to get at me at his earliest. A couple of hours late, my phone rang.

"Ayeeee, Tony, what's good, man? It's Todd. How've you been, homie?"

"Big Todd, my man!!! Aww, I been cool... can't complain, just how here trying to get it."

"I feel that, what you got going on? You playing semi-pro or overseas playing ball now?"

"Hell naw... shit after my injury, playing ball was a wrap! I'm actually involved in something I want to put you up on."

"Is that right? Okay. We need to link up and talk about it... what you doing tonight?

"I'm open, what's up?"

"Well it's CP3's birthday this weekend and we throwing him a 'lil party at Colony tonight. Why don't you come thru – I'll make sure you on the list. We can chop it up there... cool?"

"Hell yeah... I'm there!"

"Cool, I'll see you tonight."

He looks at Anna. "Baby, I need you get dressed, we're going to an exclusive NBA party."

In her Polish accent, Anna says, "Really, who's gonna be there"

"Don't worry about that," CHT says. "Just get yourself together. And nothing basic! I need you to be jaw-dropping, full-on knockout!"

Anna giggles.

CHT and Anna spend the next few hours getting ready for tonight's party. Tony decides on a grey Tom Ford suit ensemble, no tie with his grey shirt unbuttoned exposing his bare chest. He pulls out a pair of black Salvatore Ferragamo loafers from the closet to complete the outfit.

While looking at his self in the full-length mirrors, CHT mutters one word, "Boss."

Just then, the bathroom door slides open and Anna emerges. She is wearing a teal, form-fitting, low-cut, off the shoulder number that exposes her plump, bountiful breasts. Her long, blonde mane is pulled into a bun neatly on top of her head. This allows you to see her striking features and just how beautiful she is. And with her teal, tan, and pink 6-inch Christian Louboutins, Anna will stand just as tall as the NBA ballers in her company, or at least a few of them.

As CHT stares at her, he thinks to himself, "Damn, maybe I should have fucked this bitch first!" But instead of speaking his mind, he merely motions for Anna to walk towards her. He wraps his arms around her waist, pulls her close, and he whispers in her ear, "Baby, you look stunning..."

"Why, thank you..." Anna says, batting her long lashes at him.

With a kiss on her cheek, CHT says, "Fresh dressed, like a million bucks... now let's go get it!"

CHT grabs the hotel room phone and calls downstairs to the valet to request his 2013 Maserati Quattroporte be brought up. "Let's go, baby."

CHT catches Anna by her hand and they step out of the suite. As they move through the lobby, all eyes are on them. They actually appear as a new Hollywood power couple to hotel patrons. If only they knew....

As they exit the glass sliding doors of the hotel's entrance, the engine of CHT's Maserati rumbles as it's brought up front quickly. The valet jumps out and rushes to the passenger side to open the door for Anna.

"Madam," the valet says as he offers his hand to help her step into the low-slung sports car. After making sure Anna is inside, he closes her door then rushes back around to the driver's side of the car where he finds CHT already inside with his arm extended and a $20 tip awaiting him.

"Thank you, sir," the valet says, grabbing the money and closing the driver's door in one smooth motion. CHT hits the gas and peels out of the Sofitel parking lot.

At the Cabana Club, the scene is a madhouse! The valet is filled with only high-end luxury vehicle all lined up in a row: Rolls Royces, a Bentley, Lamborghinis, Ferraris, and so on.

CHT thinks to hisself, "It's on tonight!"

CHT pulls up to the valet, hands the valet attendant a $100 bill, and says, "Park my shit right here up front.... next to the white Phantom, please."

"No problem, sir," the attendant responds.

As CHT and Anna head to the entrance of this red carpet event, he confides in her how big tonight is for the both of them. As they arrive at the velvet rope, CHT gives his name and is ushered in.

"You see that baby... carte blanche! We don't wait in lines 'round here!"

Anna is clearly enamored as paparazzi cameras flash while the pair mosey into the club. This is the life she came to LA for, and within a few hours of meeting CHT, her dream has materialized.

Inside the club, music is thumping and beautiful people are having a good time. As Anna's eyes drink in the scene, she can barely control her excitement. She's never seen anything like this in her life. CHT grabs her hand and says, "C'mon, baby. I gotta find my homie Todd, the one I was telling you about."

Leading the way, CHT heads towards the VIP. He spots Todd who motions him over. "What's good, my G? Glad you could make it out."

"Man, are you kidding me? I wouldn't miss this for the world."

There are buckets of Ace of Spades champagne, Ciroc, and carafes of orange and cranberry juice.

Todd motions and ask CHT:

"You wanna drink? Go 'head! Everything is on the house tonight. We gon' EXTRA big for CP3's birthday!"

CHT tells Anna to pour them both a glass of champagne. She does. As she hands CHT his champagne, he turns back in Todd's direction while she sits down on the red crushed velvet couch.

As CHT turns, Todd looks at him wide-eyed, "Yo,

SOFITEL MACKIN' | 119

who is that bad bitch you got with you, my nigga? That bitch is bad!" Todd lets out a low whistle as he eyes Anna up and down.

CHT knew Todd would be impressed, but he didn't think he would jump on board this quick. "That's what I wanted to holla at you about, Todd... you know my injury fucked my whole career up, but I'm too addicted to a certain lifestyle, so I'm running a lil escort service. This is one of new recruits – she hasn't been in Cali more than three days. She's fresh from overseas. If you interested in her, you better get her now before the rest of these NBA niggaz do."

"Hell yeah, I'm interested! I need that tonight!"

"Well then, she's all yours." CHT turns to Anna and whispers in her ear – letting her know Todd wants to spend the rest of the evening with her. She smiles as her and CHT switch positions so she can be next to Todd. Introductions are done and Anna and Todd start in on small talk. CHT enjoys the music and more champagne while scrolling thru his iPhone.

He knows he's hit the jackpot!

After two hours of flossin' in the club, Todd lets Anna know he's ready to leave. Todd was super faded off all the liquor he consumed and horny as a muthafucka. As she grabs her clutch, CHT tells Anna to make sure she fucks the shit out of him and gets all the cash he has on him out of his pockets. She smiled, took the room keys, and led old boy out of the club. Todd slightly stumbles while heading out the club and to the valet. He's scrambling through his pockets to try and find his parking ticket.

As soon as he does, the valet grabs it and pulls his matte black Lamborghini Aventador up front. Anna's pussy gets wet as fast sports cars have always turned her on, along with the men of power that could afford them. She's prepared to pull out every stop on #18, Mr. Todd Williams starting forward for the Los Angeles Clippers.

They quickly arrive at the hotel and make their way upstairs. Todd has had his hands all over Anna on the drive over from the club. As they get on the elevator, Anna grabs Todd and shoves him against the mirrored elevator walls and begins to ravish and kiss him. She moves her hands all over his chest and down his pants aggressively grabbing his rock hard dick. It's ON!

Once off the elevator, they get to the room and are throwing their clothes off everywhere in the room. Todd falls onto the bed while Anna climbs on top of him and starts to suck his dick. She always envisioned NBA players to have bigger dicks but this will do.

That night, Anna sucked and fucked the shit outta Todd. Nothing was off limits! She licked his ass, sucked his toes, and swallowed his cum. Once the festivities were done, they both lay back on the bed. Anna glanced at the clock, which read 5:50am.

"I have to go," she said in her accented voice, while leaning over and kissing Todd on his cheek.

"Okay, baby. Lemme get you something-something." Todd reached on the side of the bed and grabbed his trousers, dug into the pockets, and pulled out a wad of $100 bills.

"When can I see you again?" Todd asked.

"Whenever you like, baby." She scribbled her number on the hotel memo pad and handed it to him. "Don't lose it!"

"Oh, I won't!"

And with that, Anna was out the door. Once on the elevator, Anna began counting the money. It was $5,000 dollars. She was overjoyed! She just lived out her fantasy and was got paid big for it! And CHT made it happen.

She pulled out her phone and called CHT.

"We good baby...?"

"Yes, daddy," she says. "Where are you?"

"I'm parked on the side of the hotel in the car, I'll pull around now."

From this point on, CHT and Anna begin to spend a lot of time together. Not because they are in love with each other but because the business was boomin'!

———————————————

"Baby, come on! The limo will be here any second to pick us up for the premiere!"

CHT is in the mirror inspecting his look before he goes to a red carpet movie premiere with Anna. He and his prized whore have broken into the Hollywood social scene and are finally enjoying the perks of their work. Tonight, along with the biggest and brightest movie stars, directors, and publicists, will be a pimp and his whore looking for multi-million dollar tricks.

Anna looks the part of the young Hollywood starlet

and she knows she will have the attention of many powerful men tonight; she loves the attention that she garners, but she knows she has to work these men to find who are willing to break bread.

Hour later, CHT's other whore Cindy, is watching the 10 o'clock news, laid up in a penthouse suite at the SLS and catches a glimpse of CHT and Anna on the red carpet being snapped by paparazzi. Cindy becomes upset and then enraged and then starts crying. She feels the anxiety welling over her and immediately calls her connect, Speedy, for a house call of something to calm her nerves.

Cindy is hurt deeply at CHT showing more attention and favor to Anna than her. She has been with CHT faithfully since they met in college. She was there for him at his lowest point in life, dealing with his career-ending knee injury, and she pulled him out of his depression and she gave herself to him as his first turn out in the pimp game and now he acts as if none of those things ever happened.

Cindy feels betrayed.

Her love for CHT has always been more than her love for herself. CHT made her feel that as long as they were together as a team that they could fight the outside world. She knew eventually there would be other hoes on the team, but she was supposed to be the bottom bitch, the anchor of CHT's operation and the most respected. It has not been like that at all.

In fact, it's the exact opposite. Anna is bringing in the most money and has all of CHT's attention and time. In truth, she is the reason that they are now in the SLS hotel right now. Cindy knows that, but she is caught up in her emotions, she feels second rate in almost every aspect of her life. Anna's arrival brought back a lot of Cindy's insecurity within herself. She knows that she is not the mainstream vision of beauty. She has known that her entire life, and that is one of the reasons she was always attracted to black men. She saw at an early age how black men would look at her thick legs, ass, and thighs. She remembers how the white boys that she thought were cute always overlooked her in school favoring the thin blondes and perky brunettes with thin legs and that thigh gap. Now with the arrival of Anna, she has been pushed to the side once again, but this time by the man she loves.

To cope with all her emotional insecurities, she started self-medicating with pills. She never used to use drugs while she was escorting. She is what the pimps call a true hoe, a woman whose sexuality allows her to turn tricks effortlessly. She chose to be a hoe willingly, but with her tricks slowing down she has a lot of free time by herself and she started taking pills as a way to distract her from feeling inadequate. She quickly became addicted to Oxycontin and Xanax, and would take any other opiate she could get her hands on. She finds all her pill deals online through Craigslist. It was on Craigslist that she met her dealer, Speedy.

Speedy is a major pill hustler. He is young, black, and has the swagger and energy that Cindy has been missing in her life from CHT. Cindy and Speedy flirt every time he drops of a delivery of pills. Tonight she wants some pills and she wants to feel Speedy inside her; she wants to feel wanted.

Cindy messages him and tells him to bring her $500 worth of pills to the SLS Hotel in Beverly Hills. He responds back promptly and confirms he will arrive within the hour. Cindy flirts in her messages to him and tells Speedy that she won't have any underwear on when he gets there and asks if he will have a problem with it. Speedy hits her back saying that she had better stop playing with him or she might get a side of dick with her order of pills. Cindy smiles; she likes the sexual attention from Speedy and it makes her feel good. She heads to the master bath to soak in the tub.

Cindy cleans herself and stares in the full-length mirror on the back of the bathroom door. She looks at her curvaceous body and finds pride in her shape as she takes a towel over body to dry off. She is excited and happy that Speedy is coming over. Her pussy becomes moist as she thinks of Speedy and the right move she can pull to get him to fuck her. It feels good to know that someone desires her. Wearing only a towel, Cindy moves to the living room and lays across the couch awaiting Speedy's delivery. After a warm, relaxing bath, Cindy dozes off.

Cindy awakes to her iPhone vibrating on the coffee table. Startled, she immediately grabs it to find she has been asleep for almost two hours and Speedy is downstairs waiting to come upstairs with her delivery. She quickly texts

Speedy the room number and he makes his way up on the elevator. Once he arrives, Speedy notices the door slightly cracked. Slowing opening the door and poking his head in the room he says, "Cindy, it's me, Speedy…. Cindy?"

"I'm here! Come on in."

"Gotdamn, girl! You was serious on not havin' any panties on! Where your clothes at, girl?!"

Cindy smiles, and seductively bites her bottom lip. She stands up, drops the towel, and says, "I need something from you, and I do not mean pills."

Speedy walks over to Cindy and starts kissing her deeply. He reaches around her waist, grabs her ass, and then pins her on the couch. He grinds on her naked body fully clothed. Cindy rubs his penis thru his Levi 501s and tugs open the buttons. She pushes him up to a standing position starts to suck and lick on hard, black dick.

Cindy loves sex, especially with a man that is well endowed! For Cindy, the only time she feels like she is bonding with a man is during sex. She uses her sexual prowess and superb oral skills to make Speedy come inside her mouth. He moans and screams and she uses tricks she learned in the game to satisfy him. She keeps his penis in her mouth and works it back to full erection. Speedy pulls his shirt off over his head, and steps out of his pants as they begin to have sex on the couch. Speedy has wanted to fuck Cindy from the first time he met her, but he didn't want to mess up their dealer/client relationship. The built up sexual tension between the two is immense and they enjoy each other for hours. Speedy's phone rings continuously as they are fucking, his customers want their drugs, but he's too wrapped up in Cindy's sex game. He turns her over on the couch in a doggie style position and begins to long stroke her out. With her long blonde mane in his fist, he starts slapping her ass with every stroke. She moans with pleasure and Speedy starts talking dirty to her.

"Take this black dick, bitch!"

"You love this dick, don't you?"

Cindy shows her appreciation simultaneously by moaning, "Yeesssss, daddy!" while squirting all over his hard dick.

That only turns Speedy on more as she can feel his dick get harder and he continues turning her on with his dirty talk:

"Yeah, cum on that dick..."

"Look at that... awwww shit!"

As Speedy tightens the grasp on her hair, he begins to thrust harder and faster in Cindy's hot pussy. He can feel her cummin' over and over as he goes faster and harder, faster and harder and harder. And with a loud grunt, Speedy cums inside of Cindy

"Uggghhhhhhh... yeah... YEAH!!!"

They both collapse on the coach, and while lying closely embracing each other, Speedy picks up his phone. "Damn, I got thirty missed calls. Cindy, I'm going to have to be out, I need to handle my biz!"

Cindy has her head on Speedy's chest. She looks

him and the eyes and says, "Go get your money, baby, I am definitely not going to stop that. I just want you to know I needed that dick from you really bad! You made me feel so good and I want to thank you for that, Speedy."

"You ain't gotta thank me for shit, Cindy! I been wantin' to fuck that thick body of yours since I first met you, shit, just ask one of my niggas and they will tell you how I always talk about you as my most official customer, both in the looks and finance department!"

As Speedy puts his clothes on, he reaches in his pants and throws Cindy her package. "This one is on me, Cindy! You always been a good customer and this is my way of sayin' that I appreciate you and the fact that you sucked and fucked the shit out of me !"

Cindy laughs and walks Speedy to the door. She kisses him before he walks out. She lingers by the door while his cum runs down her leg; she is still high on her sexual and emotional ride with Speedy.

For the first time in a long time, she thinks of a life outside of CHT and escorting.

11

STRAPZ, YOU M DUBBIN OR WHAT?

The culmination of Strapz and J Loc's adventures on the road comes as the BET Awards begin in Los Angeles. Strapz is now an official M Dub Crip and has been promoting the set through his lyrics, videos, merchandise, and concert appearances.

But while he and J Loc have been on the road profiting off of Crippin' through rapping, a deadly Crip on Crip war has escalated in Mid City.

Now, Strapz is the most famous and biggest M Dub target in America. With every major Black star and their entourage in town for the BET Awards, the streets of LA are bustling with gang members, killers, and jack artists looking to score on any artists caught slippin'.

J Loc is finally back in his beloved City of Los Angeles. It has almost been a month, but in the streets of Los Angeles a month is equivalent to six months, that's just how fast things move. The rapper life is not for J Loc. He has unintentionally become an Internet celebrity by shooting several rival gang members in Pittsburgh at a Strapz show. For the remainder of the tour, he was supposed to lay low to avoid being seen by law enforcement but that didn't work either. At the last show in Milwaukee, he had to tie up and knock around the son of a local gang leader who was holding Strapz and his entourage hostage. J Loc's whole logic to going on the tour was to get a break from the madness in the streets but it turned out to be the exact opposite. Now his little homies in his gang are emailing and texting the footage of the J Loc shooting to each other and to their gang enemies as a sign of what will happen to them by messing with the Mid City Westside Gangsta Crips. It is only a matter of time before LAPD connects the dots and starts their investigation.

J Loc, Strapz, and Lover Boy are in the living room of Strapz's Malibu mansion. Strapz is as happy as can be. His tour has generated more buzz for him than anything in the last few years. He is now officially the hottest rapper in the game again.

Strapz lights a blunt, takes a pull, and passes it to J Loc. "J Loc, Cuz, I really fucks with you, homie! You came through so many times on the tour! I owe you my life and my rep, nigga! You got me buzzin' on Twitter, YouTube, and TMZ all on some gangsta shit!"

"It ain't shit, Cuz! I'm just M Dubbin and gangsta movin', Cuz! But I'm back home now and I know tha Ones is gon' be on me fo' that shootin'! Niggas got my face all ova the place. It's just a matta of time befo' Eat'em Up or one of tha gang units recognize me!"

"Don't trip! I got the bread to help you out on anything! I got my attorneys on deck! You just took my career ova the edge! Nigga, do you know tha first thing that

Tarantino asked me when I had tha meeting with him?"

"Naw, what he say, Cuz?"

"Who in tha fuck is that guy that shot at those guys in Pittsburg? Cuz, you are a fuckin' phenomenon right now! He said the scene looked like it was right out of an action movie. If charges come down, my lawyers gon' man up."

"Ok, that's what's up! If it's all right, I'm just gon' stay out here in Malibu until the heat die down in tha hood! Since I been gone on tour, tha Deuces and tha lil homies gon' at it! I'm way too hot to be ova there right now, Cuz!"

"Nigga, that's perfect! I want you around me 24/7. I can trust you! As you saw in Milwaukee, my security is only gonna do so much, I need that real hitta around and I got some dough for you, too, yo!"

"You know I can't say no to that, Cuz!"

"We finna hit Hollywood hard this week... BET parties gon' be off the chain!! Me, you, and Lova Boy – all access, red carpet, the whole shit!"

J Loc looks at him for a moment, then says, "Strapz, shit is real ugly right now on the streets in Mid City! Niggas is gettin' killed on sight mando! If niggas see us when we out, they gon' get at me!"

"Cuz, I ain't worried about shit I'm rollin' wit' tha M Dubs! Gangstas Movin' on that trey!"

Slightly worried at Strapz's ignorance about his warning, J Loc still responds, "On tha trey, Cuz!"

◾────────────────────────────◾

Damu has been monitoring the escalating situation between

the Westside Deuces and the Mid City Westside Gangsta Crips and sees an opportunity to rid his hands of one of his worst enemies. Damu went to elementary and junior high school with a lot of Westside Deuces and has a few homies who call shots over there. In the world of gangbanging in Los Angeles, early relationships derived in the public school era create lasting treaties and necessary alliances between enemies. Damu never had problems with the Deuces in school because there were always more BPS Bloods than Deuces. He would only attack them if conflict arose but he mostly left them alone. Now he is meeting with them on getting rid of a mutual problem.

"Whad up, Damu? You good, my nigga?"

"What's up Deuce Loc? Yeah, I am all good! I am glad you could meet me over here at the Grove. Come on, let's go to the Cheesecake Factory."

"Yeah, homie! I'm hungry than a muthafucka!"

"I see you still eat like you did back in school!"

"Shit, that ain't gon' neva change!"

While walking over to the restaurant, Damu begins to discuss the reasoning on meeting. "I been hearing about and seeing what's been going on between the Deuces and The Mid Citys lately and I wanna help y'all give them the business."

"Well, nigga, talk to me. Whatchu got in mind?"

"I will give the Deuces weapons and fifty thousand dollars to take Strapz out."

"Fifty racks, Cuz? To take out a fake New York rap

nigga getting fame off OUR gangbang shit! Nigga, you know we wit' that!"

"You know I have the Blood Alliance in line and we are obliterating anything that gets in our path. I have never had a problem with the Deuces and I will make sure that everyone involved respects my word and we'll create a silent treaty with the Deuces. I can also give you my wholesale price on the cocaine plug we have which will make Deuces the only Crip gang in LA with the low ticket on a bird. You can make millions of dollars if you operate it right."

"Hell yeah! Say no more... I'm with it!"

"Strapz and his affiliation to the M Dubs is putting too much unwanted attention on what is happening in the streets on the westside. I have a few inside connects at law enforcement and I was told that they are starting a federal investigation on the shooting in Pittsburgh. If we take him out, they will be so focused on his murder that things will cool out over here and take some of this police pressure off every gang on the westside!"

"Fa'sho Damu! Let's order this food, a nigga is starvin'! But yeah, you let me know when you ready to move and we gon' make it happen."

"I want everything to go down during the BET Awards. If we do it right, it will look like a random act of violence and not gang related. We don't want the Feds to start any investigation in on us!"

"Riiiight, say no more. I gotchu, Cuz!"

The waitress returns to the table to take Damu and

Deuce's order. Damu has the Crispy Chicken Tenders with Mashed Potatoes and Deuce orders the Bar-B-Que Chicken Pizza.

And just like that, over lunch, a hit is ordered.

BET weekend in Los Angeles is the culmination of every element of urban entertainment culture converging at one place and at one time. It is the best and the worst that modern Black culture has to offer. LAPD is always on tactical alert during the BET Awards weekend because celebrities are out and about with piles of cash and high-end jewelry and easy targets to become victims of rogue robberies. While they view the event as a time to celebrate and mingle with their contemporaries, they tend to disregard the criminal element in the city and that's when they get caught slippin'. If something is gonna happen, this would be the weekend for it.

Strapz is the talk of the town at this year's BET Awards. The whole industry is abuzz with his name because of the controversy surrounding his recent front page news stories.

Strapz has been doing interviews and talking to the media all weekend and is scheduled to close out the awards show and host the largest afterparty in Hollywood that night. While out and about, Strapz has been introducing Lover Boy to the world as his new artist and J Loc has been with them in the background, low-key, blending in with Strapz's security.

They are celebrating the success of the weekend

by having a closed shopping session at Flight Club, the premiere sneaker shop in Los Angeles. The three of them try on and purchase the hottest, most exclusive kicks Flight Club offers while security stands on watchful guard outside.

But in spite of the jovial nature of the weekend, J Loc has a bad feeling that he cannot deny. The war with the Westside Deuces has stepped up lately and he has not been able to participate. He has been talking to Strapz's lawyer on what to do and a strategy, when and if charges are brought against him. The lawyer has informed him to keep a low profile until the matter blows over. As of now, he has no warrant for his arrest but it may come at any time.

But without his presence and leadership in his hood, the Mid City Westside Crips have taken several losses in the back-and-forth gunplay with the Deuces. J Loc has been talking to his homies daily and is disturbed to hear about the Deuces coming into their hood with heavy artillery and more manpower. Before J Loc left, the Deuces were on their last leg as a gang and now they have more weapons and members than ever. J Loc knows that something is not right. He knows that some outside force is supplying the Deuces with guns, but he just doesn't know who.

Lover Boy is geeked to be running around with Strapz during the BET weekend. Lover Boy in Flight Club is like a kid in a candy shop, "Cuz, these blue Jordan III joints is fiya, homie! Lemme get these in a size eleven!"

Strapz notices J Loc is unreceptive and distant to the current scene. "J Loc, what's wrong wit' you, Cuz? You ain't fuckin' wit' none of the shoes?"

"Naw, we just got a gang of shit from that gift suite in Hollywood. I'm good, Cuz! As a matter of fact, I need to hit this blunt outside! I'm gonna step outside fo' a minute!"

"Yeah, aight! Me and Lova Boy is in here gettin' it on!"

J Loc steps outside, stands between two bodyguards, and lights up a blunt. He has been smoking a lot more as of late in an attempt to mask the pressure that's got him stressin'. But to J Loc, that's a sign of weakness. In his mind, whatever gon' come, gon' come. He just has to handle it as it does.

J Loc stands there on Fairfax watching the cars go by on the densely populated fashion-forward street. Even though he is on the outskirts of Mid City and ten minutes away from his hood, he still feels a sense of uncertainty. J Loc pulls from his blunt and shakes his head, thinking to himself, "This rap shit really ain't for me."

J Loc is ready to go back to the underground world of gang banging and wants to leave the unwanted attention to Strapz. He puts out the remainder of the blunt out and moves towards the door to go in when someone yells out his name in a passing car.

"Fuck you, Kid Titties! Niggas gon' kill you, J Loc!"

Instinctively, J Loc hits the ground. A round of gunfire comes from the car hitting one of the bodyguards. J Loc takes his gun from his waist and he and the other bodyguard fire back. The car moves northbound on Fairfax and quickly exits the scene. The front of the store has been riddled with bullets and there is glass everywhere in the aftermath of the shooting.

J Loc pats his body off and runs into Flight Club. He knows that the war with the Deuces is spilling into the award weekend activities and bodies are about to drop. "Cuz, we gotta go! LAPD is gon' be here in a minute and start questionin' niggas! I'm outta here wit' one of tha trucks! It was some busta ass dookies, Cuz, I saw them niggas!"

J Loc dashes outside with a bodyguard and jumps into a SUV and they roar away from the scene.

Strapz and Lover Boy look at the carnage of broken glass, blood, and the smell of gunpowder. They have both seen shootings like these their whole lives. Unfazed by the drive-by Strapz calls out to the store manager, "Yo, on the real! Let me get them shoes I was lookin at, Cuz! But we gotta go! And make sure there ain't no glass or blood on them shits!"

But before Strapz and the rest of his entourage can make a move to load up and roll out, squad cars pull in from every direction. Officers arrive in the store and draw weapons on Strapz and everyone in the store.

"LAPD! Get you fuckin' hands in the air and lay face down on the ground!"

Strapz defiantly keeps counting his money to pay for his kicks at the register, and barks back at the officers, "Aye, yo fuck that! Nigga, its glass everywhere on tha floor! I'm an entertainer! I just got shot at! You muthafuckas is 'sposed to be helpin' me!"

Police rush everyone to the floor. Once they get the scene under control, they begin ushering employees outside for questioning.

One of the last ones out the door is Strapz. He is being lead outside in handcuffs by a lead detective from the robbery/homicide division.

Once placed in the back of a squad car, the officer casually says, "You want a cigarette, Strapz?"

"Yeah, yeah, I appreciate that, yo!" The policeman hands Strapz a lit cigarette. "Yo, good looking, G! Them otha cops that rushed in was mad disrespectful. Orderin' niggas to lay down on a floor with glass and blood everywhere, pullin' guns on us. We the ones that just got shot at!"

"No problem, Strapz. My kids fuckin' love your music, man!"

"That's what's up, yo! Gimme a piece of paper; I'll sign an autograph fo' yo' kids. Take that home to them, man!"

"Strapz, I really appreciate that. My kids are gonna go bananas!"

"That's nothin', my dude! What's your name, man?"

"Detective Brody, but everybody calls me Eat 'em Up on the streets."

"So what you a gang detective or something?"

"No, not at all. I work in robbery homicide on all the big profile cases. They called me in because of some intel I have that concerns you."

"What kinda info you talkin' 'bout?"

"Strapz, I have reason to believe that there is a hit out on your life. One of my confidential informants in the Westside Deuces told me that they were given fifty thousand dollars to knock you off."

"What?" Strapz sits back and takes a long drag from that cigarette. "Yo, that's crazy! Them niggas really think I'm from M Dub, huh? They wanna rub a gangsta out? Well, tell them fuck niggas, come on then! I ain't runnin' from shit, niggas been tryin' to kill me since I was twelve years old, we can just add they asses to a long list of enemies I got."

"Look Strapz, I know you are a tough guy. I know you went to jail in New York for manslaughter and you handle your business but these Crips out here are pretty fucking slimy and they are constantly killing and shooting one another. If at all possible, you may just want to stay out of the public until the BET Awards are over!"

"Look Eat 'em Up, or whatever your name is, I really appreciate you puttin' me up on tha hit, but I ain't scared of no niggas. If it's my time to go, then it's my time to go! Every day since I came home from up north has been like heaven to me anyway! I'm at the biggest point in my career right now. I'm the closest thing to a 50 Cent or Tupac that the industry has seen in years. I gotta keep gangsta movin' until the wheels fall off!"

"Do what you do Strapz, but don't say we didn't warn you, man!"

Eat 'em Up unlocks the back door and lets Strapz out.

Strapz gets out but before he shuts the door, Eat em Up says to him, "Strapz, I almost forgot. Tell your man J Loc I said what's up. Tell him we have mutual friends in Malibu and Pittsburgh!"

"Yeah whateva, I'll let him know, cop!"

Eat 'em Up waits, watches, and smokes as everyone in Strapz's entourage is released after giving reports. They pile into the remaining two trucks and head back to the house in Malibu.

As he starts his police cruiser and heads North on Fairfax, Office Brody aka Eat 'em Up makes a call on his personal cell phone.

"Hey, it's Eat 'em Up. Yeah, everything is going according to plan. That arrogant asshole Strapz is playing right into our plan. Just let me know when you want to do it so I can have the tactical escape route in order for you. He is as good as dead. And you can pay me right afterwards!"

━━━━━━━━━━━━━━━━━━━━━━━━━━━━━━━━━━

The Pacific Ocean has been the calm in the violent life of J Loc. He smokes on a blunt and watches the ocean roll into the coastline in Malibu. He is preparing to deal with the consequences of his reckless actions as a gang leader in the streets of Los Angeles and it seems as if his past has finally caught up with him.

Strapz has already alerted him that after the shooting at Flight Club that a detective named Eat 'em Up from robbery homicide is on his trail for Blue Devil's murder a few years ago and for his connection to the shootings in Pittsburgh. J Loc knows the only alternative to the life he is living is jail or death and he accepts those as his end results. He came from shit and would ultimately be shit. These are the cards he was dealt in life and he accepts them. As he blows smoke out of his nose from the blunt, he grabs the gun in his waistband and makes a promise to himself and his dead homies that he will not go down without a fight.

Strapz comes out to the back of the house with two exquisite models in bikinis where J Loc is smoking.

"Yo Loc! Its BET weekend! Fuck all that bullshit right now... relax. We here at the mansion, Cuz! Ain't nothin' goin' down if we don't want it to!" Strapz thinks he's untouchable at this point. He's on top of the world. He is the king inside of his Malibu mansion and holding court. He puts his arm around J Loc and continues. "Yo Cuz! Look around at all this! I came from nothin', Cuz! I was born in South Central on the eastside just like you! My moms was fifteen years old and from a third world country and didn't even really know my pop when she had me. I been shot, in jail for attempted murder, stabbed, and at war wit' niggas my whole life. J Loc, you saved my ass twice since I've known you! I been talkin' to my lawyer and he is on retainer to help you with the shit in Pittsburgh or whateva else the ones try to put on you, Cuz! I gotchu, my nigga!"

J Loc looks Strapz directly in his eyes and says, "Yo, I appreciate that, Strapz! That shit means a lot to me, Loco!"

"Nigga, I gotcha, homie! Don't think this is tha drink

or that I am just frontin' for the bitches, but I love you, my nigga, and you have helped me see that you can never run from tha nigga you are, Cuz. I am tired of runnin' from shit. If I die today, I lived a helluva life! One thing I picked up from you is to not give a fuck! I'm serious, Cuz! I am gonna go down in history as one of tha realest niggas who eva did it! I'm on some Pac shit now! Nigga, it's M Dubs or no love! Fuck dem Do-Dos! It's Deuce K on mine!"

Strapz motions for two of the girls to come over and they walk him into the house. J Loc gets that feeling in his stomach again that only comes when someone gets shot or killed. He continues to smoke his blunt and looks for solace once more in the heavy, crashing waves of the Pacific.

The next morning, the city is in a frenzy with BET weekend fever. The airports are crowded with tourists, groupies, and the stars arriving. The streets are filled with luxury cars and SUVs and onlookers. The LAPD presence is everywhere. They are the modern equivalent of the overseers on the slave plantation posted to overlook and suppress the movements of their valuable human cargo.

Strapz's tour bus and security bus pull into the Westside Mall for an in-store stop, promoting a new release from his clothing line.

"Damn, Cuz! It's like 500 muthafuckas out there for the in-store, Strapz!"

"I see that, Lova Boy, and now do you see that half of the crowd is bitches? I told ya, J Loc, these bitches is in love wit' my gangsta!"

"You wuz right, Cuz! Just make sure you don't bring back no more mud ducks, homie!"

Everybody on the bus laughs. J Loc looks through the crowd of fans to see if he recognizes any Westside Deuces. The tour bus pulls into the valet section of the mall and Strapz's security sets up a perimeter of cover and the entourage exits. Strapz and Lover Boy exchange the Mid City Westside Crip handshake and are rushed into the in-store.

J Loc stays with security and looks for any strange movements. Everything looks okay and the police and store security let the fans into the store to meet Strapz. Fans move in and out for an hour, taking pictures and having Strapz sign various items. Lover Boy sits right next to Strapz and even signs a few autographs himself. The store managers come over to Strapz and tell him that it is time for him to exit; the crowd is becoming a little unruly and they want to clear the store of its urban element. His security leads him and the entourage out of the store to the valet section.

The valet section is closed to the public and surrounded by police and security. J Loc is still on edge. He knows that regardless of the police presence that if a banger decides he is going to shoot or kill someone there is nothing that will stop him if he is a real G. The harder the obstacles, the more valued the kill is. He knows they are still in the eye of the storm.

The entourage waits for the tour bus to pull back up

to the valet section. Strapz and Lover Boy stand behind a wall of security. Strapz is cracking jokes and is in a jovial mood. He finally feels at home in the city of his birth. A mall security car pulls into the valet and one of the security guards asks Strapz if he can he have an autograph.

"Yeah, why not, homie? Come over here and get it!"

The security guard opens the door to come over.

"Westside Deuces Nigga! M Dub Killa!"

The driver of the mall security car and the passenger open fire with two assault rifles on Strapz and his security. Hundreds of rounds are dispensed in a flash. The barrage of bullet mows down several of Strapz's security that hasn't ducked out of the way and Strapz himself falls to the ground behind them.

J Loc jumps behind a car and gets in a defensive firing position. He pulls out both of his handguns and fires back into the mall security car.

The police officers in the valet section do nothing. They cower in fear looking for cover from the rapid succession of gunfire and call for back up to the scene.

J Loc is a gangsta. It is ingrained in him to die trying to kill his enemy. The security car rips through the valet section and turns to make a U-turn to exit. J Loc fires with precision into the car. The passenger and driver are both struck. The car veers into traffic but crashes right past the mall entrance. J Loc then runs from the mall into the streets of Los Angeles.

Fans are screaming, police sirens are in the air, and

death has arrived on the scene. Strapz's and Lover Boy's bodies lay mangled with those of security in front of the valet. Ten people are dead and twenty have been wounded. It is the worst mass shooting in Los Angeles history. Inside the crashed car are the dead bodies of two Westside Deuce members disguised as security guards. Robbery/Homicide detectives are on the scene in minutes along with the Gang Unit, ICE, FBI, and Homeland Security.

Detective Eat'em up looks at the two dead gangsters in the car and picks up his phone.

"It's done. These motherfuckers killed Strapz and about nine other people! But somebody lit these boys the fuck up. They didn't even make it away from the mall. I'm going to continue the investigation here and try to identify the bodies. Damu, I will call you again when I get out of here, which will probably be in about twelve hours. Just let me know where to pick up my money."

12

THE FEDS IN TOWN

"This is Steve Whiteman reporting live and direct from Los Angeles in the Mid City as Federal agents, Homeland Security, and local law enforcement agencies wage war in the streets against westside street gangs. As you see, it almost has a riot like feel as authorities are moving in tanks and military Humvees in anticipation of retaliatory combat from these domestic terrorists."

Brazyiak and Damu could not believe what they were seeing and had never seen anything like this. When the '92 riots happened, we were both just babies, but now on live TV they sat transfixed, watching a Federal military take over. It was like looking at Iraq or Afghanistan except it is up the street on Pico and La Brea. They have already started to head to Damu and Brazyiak's neighborhood, and because of that fact, they have been hiding in Little Ethiopia with some Ethiopian homies from the hood.

Brazyiak is on the Top 30 most wanted gangster list along with every other Blood leader on the westside except Damu. But there is already suspicion growing in the streets on why Damu is not on the list.

In the streets of Los Angeles, gangsters are killed daily over gossip, innuendo and jealousy without a lick of evidence or proof. So imagine the scrutiny that Damu is being placed under with his omission from the list. All the streets need to kill is assumption and innuendo, and with Damu not being on the list, he looks like he is working with law enforcement to the streets.

The streets are saying he is working with the Feds or why else would one of the most powerful Blood leaders in the city not be on the list? The streets are asking questions and soon Damu will have to answer back with either his words or his blood, or both.

———————————————————————

Meanwhile on the Crip side....

J Loc is still reeling from the murders of Strapz and Lover Boy and the attempted assassination on his life. He is far from his hood in Palisades and deciding which of his enemies to attack first when he receives a phone call.

"Yeah, whadd up? Yeah I'm near a TV, Cuz. Hold up. You screaming and I can't undastand you!"

J Loc turns on the TV and drops his phone after seeing his hood being overcome by local law enforcement and federal troops. He picks up the phone and talks to his homie. "Damn, Cuz, look what these crackers done did to the hood! They fuckin' smoked Big BK, Lil Light Blue, and Locy Loc with them raids! What the fuck am I gonna do? Cuz, Imma call you when I leave from this bitch tilt on the hood, Crip!"

If J Loc wasn't fucking a white bitch out in Palisades, he would be fucked up or even dead right now. But he was still fucked 'cuz he had to get out of this all-white area and get around some kinda niggas and blend in.

J Loc took one last drag on his blunt as he slipped out the door thinking, "They got my face blasted all ova TV between Strapz's murder and on this bullshit Most Wanted thirty list as they tear my hood up. And niggas ask why I don't go to church. If God was real, then why is this shit happening to me and my people? Man, we just some niggas in the hood tryin' to survive. We was born into this war and now they got us out here like terrorists. I gotta lay low but I need to be near the hood to see and hear what these Feds is doin'. I'm seriously contemplating takin' my heat and just shootin' it out with these Woods until I die! What the fuck I got to live for? My hood crushed Momma and Daddy dead and I'm on the run for my life. I got some homies in Little Ethiopia and it's close to the hood, but in the cut. Let me wake this bitch up and get on the move! On Crip, I'm fighting Slobs, police, and anybody in my way until I get smoked out here."

13

In the Real with Damu

Should I just blow my fucking brains out, homie?

Really, can shit get any worse than what it is right now?

Living the life of a fugitive on the run is driving me insane, Blood.

And If I'm thinking like this in my mind, I can only imagine what Brazyiak's thinking in his demented thoughts.

Brazyiak and I have been hiding out, stuck together in this small apartment 24 hours a day for the last two weeks now. The federal takeover of the westside of Los Angeles has forced us to stay put. There is no way for us to make any moves without fear of being arrested or shot on sight by law enforcement.

We have not been able to do anything but eat Ethiopian take-out food and watch the news as they cover the feds attacking every known gang neighborhood that ever existed on the westside.

I'm just—I don't know, man. I guess I am getting what they call cabin fever, just getting really nervous and antsy. I haven't had to be this still and immobile since I was convicted of a shooting and sentenced to Youth Authority. Those YA fools kept me locked down while I was in there.

I swore to myself when I was locked down then that if I ever got out of those conditions that I would be as active as humanly possible. I have been able to keep my word on that until now and this situation.

All I did up until now was think as I moved. I am constantly forming and restructuring ways to make the Blood Alliance work better. It does not matter much what I am doing in life, whether fucking a female or planning a mission to eliminate an enemy. I am always thinking on how to make the Blood Alliance work. But along with that continual thought, I am also in perpetual action so it doesn't seem obsessive or even a dominant thought.

It is for me a driving thought of motivation.

But now with things the way they in the westside with the Feds on our back and me having to put my operations to a standstill, I've been forced to grind to a halt. The only thing that is still moving is my mind and it is driving me up the wall! I am trying to slow down once again like I did in jail and concentrate. Damn, all this is taking me back to when I arrived at YA.

I was incarcerated in YA for ten long years, Blood. They call that serving a YA life sentence. I became the man I am today through serving that bid.

My entire adolescence and young adulthood were formed by doing hard time in the California Penal system. I entered at 12 years old and came out at 22. I was released a day before my 23rd b-day. My original sentence was supposed to extend from YA to Pelican Bay once I turned 21, but Allah had other plans for me.

My father paid for the best appellate lawyer in the country and he arranged for my release on appeal. If it was not for my father doing that, I was supposed to have served another fifteen years to life. But my father, in one of his rare moments of giving a fuck about someone other than his self, really worked that situation out for me and got everything turned over for me on that appeal.

I have never forgotten the fact that I was given a second chance at life.

But in all honesty, I have to ask myself: *what have I really done with that second chance?* I am still murdering people and still engulfed in a life of crime. I am doing nothing to honor my Lord or make the world a better place through my freedom.

What the fuck is wrong with me? I hate to admit it, but as much as I hate my selfish ass father for the things he has done to me, I am a lot like him. Something deep inside me just went haywire long ago and I have been trying to fix it ever since.

The only thing that makes me feel remotely good is thinking about the Blood Alliance and at this point, what does that even mean now with every Blood leader on the westside thinking that I am cooperating with the feds? All I can do now is stare at the wall above me, just like I did back in those YA days.

I went into YA with five counts of murder and five attempted murder counts on my jacket. The big homies who caught the charges with me are all on death row and are both facing their last stays of execution this year. Those were my guys, Blood. Big Way Back and Crip Killer Bill. They have been off the streets for fifteen years. Their lives have been frozen in time, thanks to the State of California. Allah knows how I love the homies! They were the only form of guidance I had growing up in the Jays.

We made nationwide news on the shootings because of my age and the fact that it was ten people shot and five people killed. If I close my eyes, I can remember everything like it was yesterday.

I was in the sixth grade and school had just let out for the day. I had gotten off the school bus and went directly home to Uncle Mo's pad in the hood.

This was during the height of gang activity in LA so as soon as I went in the house at Uncle Mo's, I grabbed his 9mm Browning for protection, checked myself in the mirror, and headed to the neighborhood McDonald's on La Brea and Rodeo to get something to eat.

As soon as I walked into that McDonald's, I could feel tension and animosity.

There were three tables full of Crabs staring down everybody in the restaurant. I couldn't believe my eyes. I had never seen that many Crabs that close to the jays ever. I would find out later during my trial that one of their Crab homies had recently gotten smoked and they were having a car wash to raise money for his dusty ass funeral.

They were en route back to their hood and I guess they figured that since they were so deep they would loc out in the first Blood neighborhood they encountered, which was mine.

It was a bad idea for those niggas.

They were Mid Cities aka Kid Titty Sexside Crabs.

I looked up from the counter ordering my food as more of these fools pulled their low riders in a circle and started bumping their sounds and hopping their cars in the parking lot. My senses were tingling before I could even get the food that I had just ordered at the counter.

I saw the two big homies who are always on patrol at the McDonald's, Big Wayback and Crip Killer Bill, confronting these niggas in the parking lot out front. I didn't even think about shooting, I just went into action in that split second.

It would be at that moment of action and not thinking that would change my young life forever. In a three-second decision, I ran out of the McDonald's with my gun and started firing at the Crabs to help my big G's.

I wanted to show these Crabs they couldn't disrespect me, my hood, or my homies the way that they were. But I also wanted a release for all the anger that was pent up in me from my mother dying, my father leaving me, and just feeling abandoned and this was it.

I pulled out the gun and started dumping on the Crabs outside and when the Crabs came from inside the restaurant, I shot at them, too. I let off, the big homies let off, and the Crabs let off. The whole parking lot erupted in gunfire.

Bullets were flying in every direction.

When the shooting was finally over, five Crabs were smoked and three Crabs were hit, as well as two Bloods. The police came quickly because of the amount of gunshots and surrounded us. We were arrested before we could flee the scene. There was so much gun play during the shootout that we could not move and we were forced to take position. When we did try to escape, the Ones were everywhere.

There was nowhere for us to run to. I lost everything that I knew in the first twelve years of my life in under thirty minutes. I was now property of the State of California.

There was so much media coverage on the shooting so quickly that by the time I was detained and brought into juvenile detention, I was already a star among the inmates. I realized early on that I could use the shooting to my advantage. All the Bloods in detention center fell in line under me as their new leader.

I mean niggas that were seventeen and eighteen years old were looking at me, a twelve-year-old year old child, to tell them what G moves to make.

I ran with it.

I did a whole year before sentencing. I accepted my new position as a shotcaller in jail and prepared for my court date and prepared for the worst because of all the media attention.

I was right to do so.

The homies came to court acting brazy for the cameras. They had become even more celebrated than me in the County jail and were now looked at as two of the most powerful Bloods in the California penal system. They ate up all the attention from the media. They were banging our set and talking loud to the cameras and being as disruptive as they possibly could.

The judge in our case hated that and scorned all of us as he gave all three of us life sentences. Big Wayback threw his shoe at the judge and yelled out "Crab Killer!" I fell out laughing, but truthfully, that would be one of the last times I would laugh in years.

I did most of my sentence at the YA camp in the Valley at Sylmar. The time went by really quick because I was so young. I organized the Bloods into an aligned movement under my program. We checked every Crab that came in and got at any Ese that disrespected the B.

Since I speak Spanish fluently, I would hear the Eses talking shit out loud about the Blacks and ruin their plans for any action on us with a preemptive attack on them.

Uncle Mo would come through to see me and he would always bring a Quran and Hadith. He kept the Muslim part of me alive and eventually that side of me took over more so than the gang banger side.

I was born a Muslim, but I didn't get on the Deen until I was locked up. Inside jail, I would organize Jummah on Friday with the homies and we would get the Imam from

Masjid Abu Bakr by the hood to give the Khutbah. For the first time in my life, I had a sense of balance and peace. But I was still locked up. I hated the fact that my freedom was not mine to fully control.

And that's how I feel now on the run. Just thinking about all the turmoil that I have been through has given me a better sense of what to do next. I have to think of a way to shake the Feds and clear my name on these streets with the Bloods. But how?

14

Niggas love Grape Soda

Blood, I been in a lot of trouble in my nineteen years on the planet, but I ain't neva seen nothin' like this shit that me and Damu is in right now, Blood. I am officially one of the Most Wanted niggas in America right now! Me, Blood!

As wild as it sounds, I'm half way proud of that shit and that shit lets all the Gs in the LA know the business on Brazyiak from that mad-ass Westside Gangsta Blood! I been reachin' for that infamy in the streets of LA since I was a youngsta and I finally have it.

But then on the other hand, I got every One time and Federal in the bity lookin' for yo' boy. Blood, we deep underground. All my spots done been hit up by the Feds. Moms, all my pollos, my main whoop... shit, they shook the hood down hard and got every active nigga from Westside Gangsta Bloods in jail or on the run. But me and Damu ain't yo' average gangstas, Blood!

It's gon' take a whole lot to bring us down, homie, and we ain't goin' nowhere wit'out a fight! We linked up with some Ethiopian Bloods from Damu's hood and we been posted up in Little Ethiopia since.

We still westbound and five minutes away from my

hood or Damu's hood, so at least there's that.

We been on the low for two weeks now. Damu is still just as solid as ever but I can tell Blood is hurtin' like a muthafucka by how these niggas done turnt on him. All that work we been puttin' in to keep the Bloods on top thru the Blood Alliance and niggas just flip like a burger wit' no paperwork or nothin' on Damu.

The Blood Alliance is damn near broke up and ain't nobody feelin' nobody in these streets right now. It's just too much misinformation, snitchin' and police raids goin' on. Every day niggas is goin' down and the Feds done forced niggas hands out here just to survive. Some putos and Westside Deuce Crabs tried to go at the Feds the first week of the Fed takeover and sixty motherfuckers got killed in raids and arrests.

They wiped out both of they muthafuckin' hoods, them shits don't exist no mo'. That shit looked like Iraq on TV! LA ain't never seen nothin' like this, not even with the two riots that happened before.

As I have said all my life, fuck it, Blood, you gon' go when it's your time to go so you might as well do what you gon' do until then!

I ain't got time to be scared, and shit, I gotta survive any muthafuckin' way I can Blood. We got two K's, three Glocks, and a ASR in the apartment we stayin' in.

We been eatin' straight takeout from different Ethiopian spots the whole time we been layin' low. Blood, I am so sick of that shit that I would kill a nigga over a cheeseburger, B.

Brazyiak yells, "Dog, I'm going brazy eatin' this soggy ass shit, Blood! I need some chili cheese fries and a grape soda in this bitch. Look Damu, we low on food and I'm tired of eating this foreigner shit, Blood! I got the glasses and the wig and that hat you gave me to disguise myself 'cuz, Blood, I gotta get some fast food in me or I'm gon' die. I can bend one and hit that Carl's on the corner and be back in a minute, Blood!"

Damu calmly responds to Brazyiak, "Blood, you know that's not a good idea. The Feds are out there everywhere and anything that looks even slightly suspicious is going to peak their attention. I think we should just continue to lay low, my YG." Brazyiak sinks back into the couch, looking defeated. "But if you have to get out for a minute and stay in disguise, Brazyiak, I will make an exception to the rules and you can go out. But make it a quick one, two Brazyiak. I will watch the gate to make sure you're not followed or tracked, Blood!"

Brazyiak jumps up with excitement. He has been cooped up for too long and he needs to move outside the confines of the apartment hideout.

He smiles and exclaims to Damu, "On Bloods, homie, you know I love you like the brotha I never had, but if you wasn't gon' let me go, we was gonna catch a heavy fade!"

Damu and Brazyiak both laugh out loud. For the first time since they have been on the run, Damu and Brazyiak express a form of emotion not associated with their life on the run. Brazyiak grabs his tools for disguise and heads to the bathroom to prepare for his fast food run.

Damu grabs the Glock from the coffee table in the living room and gets ready to walk Brazyiak down to the front gate of the apartments. He doesn't feel good about letting Brazyiak walk to Carl's Jr, but he knows he must do it to keep things between him and Brazyiak on good terms.

Leaders are only as good as the people that follow them and Damu understands that you must at times relinquish to your followers' wishes and show them that you too can follow their direction as well. Damu also feels with almost certainty that something bad is about to happen. Brazyiak emerges from the bathroom in full disguise and heads towards the front door.

He looks at Damu and says, "Let's ride out, Blood, I'm ready!"

They both head downstairs to the main gate of the apartments.

Brazyiak throws up the B with his fingers and the W for his set and walks off in the direction of Carl's Jr. Damu stands inside the gate watching as his best friend and closest comrade walks way.

He still can't shake the feeling that something bad is about to happen.

15

ENEMIES?

At the Carl's Jr, Brazyiak runs into his rival J Loc.

"What's up Crab?"

"You know the biz, muthafucka!"

"You Slob piece of shit!"

Both of them with their hands on their pistols, Brazyiak and J Loc stand in front of the drive-thru window of Carl's Jr on the corner or Olympic and Fairfax in the heart of Little Ethiopia ready to shoot each other to death. Both of them on the run from the Feds, both in disguise, and both know that their freedom and lives will be changed forever if either pull out their guns.

"Blood, I wanna kill your Crab ass so bad!"

"But I'll catch you, Kid Titties!"

And with that Brazyiak runs down the alley towards the hideout.

With each step he takes dashing down the alley, Brazyiak sees his young life flash before his very eyes. He knows he may have ruined his and Damu's chances of freedom. Thoughts move as rapid as his feet and legs.

From years of gang-banging and police pursuit, he knows how to evade anyone and not be followed directly to where he is headed.

It's almost like a part of his DNA. He hops one gate goes through a backyard jumps over a fence lands on his feet and runs in a circle to throw anybody off his trail. With his heart pounding, he kneels by a back house and waits to see if J Loc or any cops or Feds come down the main alley in pursuit of him.

Taking this opportunity to gain his composure he removes his sweatshirt and wipes the beads of sweat dripping from his face and neck. After three minutes, he knows it's now or never and he dashes down the alley to the apartment complex where he and Damu are lying low.

He spots J Loc in the apartment complex coming through the opposite entry. He has the drop on J Loc and can smoke him easily because J Loc is looking behind him to see if anyone followed him to his hideout.

Brazyiak thinks to himself, "I should just kill this Crab now and take my chances with the Feds when they come! Fuck it Blood, I gotta stay movin'!"

But in that split second, J Loc looks up and sees Brazyiak scoping him. They glance at each other eyeball to eyeball. It is the stare of warriors, soldiers, and killers on the streets of Los Angeles. No words could ever properly convey the look of murder and the predator on the hunt.

But before either can pull out their weapons, Damu jumps between both of them.

"On Stones, homie, don't do it! We cannot risk our freedom over this nigga! Brazyiak, we cannot do it like this, not right now, nigga! Just us standing out here is bringing attention. If you shoot each other, the gunfire will bring out the Feds for sure!"

"Nigga just move out!"

"Fuck y'all niggas, Cuz! I ain't goin' nowhere, let the pigs come! Fuck it! I've been stayin' over here with the homie from By Yourself Crip for a week and I'm tired of runnin' and creepin' from muthafuckas. Nigga, fuck y'all, this Crip hood!"

"So what Crab?"

"We been over here for two weeks and it's a Blood hood now, bitch! Youse a dumb ass nigga. My homie Damu tryin' to save ya life and you wanna loud talk us!"

Damu tries to make peace saying, "You niggas chill. We have to get out of this courtyard screaming or someone is definitely going to call the police!"

J Loc's homie from By Yourself Crip comes outside his apartment with his hand on his waistline showing his weapon. "Whaddup, Loco?"

"On Crip, these niggas is slobs, Cuz! Not regular slobs either, I'm mean super Slobs Cuz! This is that nigga Damu I was tellin' you 'bout from Wacc Piss Stones that's got all the Slobs in line togetha!"

"What is it then Crip?"

The By Yerself Hustler Crip puts his hand on his heat in his waistline and looks at J Loc for the order to pull it out.

Damu knows if he doesn't make the right move in a few seconds, he will be involved in a shootout for his life with the Crips and then the Feds will show and he will never see his Blood Alliance come to pass or his freedom again.

He must take dire measures.

"Look man, we are all on the run from the Feds. Gun play is going to guarantee that the Feds are going to come this way and whoever isn't dead from the gunfight is going to be in jail for the rest of their lives. We have to agree to disagree and do it later! We are moving to where we are staying at and you go your way and we will handle this like gangsters when time permits, J Loc!"

And with that both parties run to their respective hideout apartments.

The countdown to confrontation has just started.

Damu can't believe his bad luck and ponders to himself, "Today I saw my freedom once again flash before my eyes. Something told me not to let Brazyiak go to that fucking Carl's Jr, but I relented as the big homie and let him go anyway. Once he gets to Carl's Jr, Brazyiak runs into one of our worst enemies, Crab ass J Loc from Kid Titties. These two damn near have a shootout right on Olympic in front of the Carl's Jr. After both of them flee the spot from Carl's Jr and evade law enforcement, they both end up escaping to the same apartment complex to hideout!

I can't believe that shit. The same apartment complex where we both have been staying at! We've been here for two weeks and this Crab has been right downstairs from us for who knows how long! Little Ethiopia isn't an official hood, it is an open turf so anyone can try and move around here, but don't fuck with the Ethiopians and keep a low profile and this should be a nice area close to the hood for us to lay low. We're over here in the first place because we have a few little homies that bang Blood over here and they were able to tuck us away.

Now on the other side of the coin there is a set of Ethiopian Crabs in the Palms section of West Los Angeles called the By Yer Self Hustler Crips and since this is their cultural homeland, I guess a few of them are over here pushing a Crip line, too. Now at this juncture with the Crabs, time and circumstance have forced us to agree to disagree or it is literally over for all of us.

Law enforcement are everywhere on the westside because of the Federal takeover and we cannot afford to make any sudden movements or have any shootouts or they will be all over here. Any gangbangers who are from the westside and haven't already got caught up in the Federal takeover are all laying as low as possible So now we play the waiting game while I try to figure out how to get us out of this mess.

All of our destinies lie in each other's hands. My life is being determined by the idiotic and irrational thoughts of some Crabs! I have to be as analytical and strategic as I can be or Brazyiak and I are dead meat. One wrong move and it is over for all parties involved." As he thinks through all this, Damu rubs his head in frustration and closes his eyes with the gravity of the situation.

Brazyiak looks at Damu still sitting with his eyes closed. "Look Blood, before you even start, Damu, let me explain what happened! That Crab nigga just popped up outta nowhere at Carl's. It was not my fault! I didn't start shit wit' him, Damu. In fact, I ran! Let's murk these niggas and shake the spot, Blood. I'm not sure where we gon' go, but I'm working on that if we stay here even if the police don't get us, the rest of them Crabs is gon' try to creep on us homi. We just up here like sittin' ducks, Blood, waitin' fo' them to make a move!"

Damu thinks carefully before he speaks. "Brazyiak, listen to me, homie. I am not blaming you for anything that's happening, but we are in an almost no-win situation! If we smoke those Crabs, we are as good as caught with all the Feds in the area. And at this point, who's to say that we are not being monitored or under surveillance now?"

As Damu speaks, he looks out the window downstairs to see at least three new Crabs go into the apartment where J Loc and the Ethiopian Crabs are. They are planning something or about to make a move. Damu has that feeling in his stomach that only comes with involvement in gun play and violence.

———————————————————————

At the same time, downstairs with J Loc and the Ethiopian Crip set BYSH....

"Cuz, them Slobs upstairs are two of my set's worst enemies! On M Dubs, I wanna smoke them Slobs right muthafuckin' now, Cuz! I'm madda than a muthafucka I didn't kill them niggas, Cuz, but I know as soon as I did it the Ones was gon' come thru here and air it out and that can't happen, Cuz. I'm tha last nigga from my click still ridin' out here. But I wanted to get some back up in case they got turnt up so I'm glad y'all came thru, Cuz, but I'm lettin' niggas know if them Slobs do anythang outta pocket Cuz, I'm goin' down shootin' them niggas and the Ones!" The leader of the BYSH Crips looks a little shook at his words and rubs his head in frustration. No one wants to bring those feds over here and with all this, J Loc is bringing to much attention to their low-key hideout.

Damu doesn't know it but Brazyiak has made a call and some of the 5th Ave Blood homies come over as backup and bring some extra heat with them. It just feels like something bad is gonna happen.

It is now a matter of time and emotion that will tell who makes the next move as tension builds with both sides.

We now see both groups of gangsters on the edge with heavy artillery, paranoia, and hatred for one another. The next logical step is violence of some sort. Damu speaks to his partner, "Brazyiak, we are going to have to do something major to get us out of this predicament, homie. I mean something out of order for us to get out of this jam."

"Well, you the brains of this shit. What you gon' do, Blood? Whatever it is I got ya back, B!"

"I am going to call Councilman Lopez. He owes us big time for not giving me any warning on the Fed takeover and now it's time to cash in on that favor."

"I don't know about that dude, Blood. He was on

the Blood payroll and didn't let nobody know about none of this Fed shit when it went down. I don't trust that beana for shit!"

"Yeah, yeah. I feel you on that, homie, but if he doesn't come through with helping us out, then on Stones the last thing I do before I get smoked by the Feds is shoot Lopez in his motherfucking head, Blood." Damu reaches in his pocket and pulls out one of his two burner cell phones that cannot be traced by signal. He looks out the front window of the apartment window to see if there is any activity from downstairs with the Crips. All seems quiet. For now.

He dials. "Lopez."

"Hello, who is this?"

"It is Damu!"

There is an eerie silence, and then he starts dragging. "Damu... uhhmm, I didn't recognize your voice at first... listen about the Injunction, um, there was nothing I could..."

Damu interjects and cuts him off. "Lopez, I am not in the mood for any of your politician bullshit. I need to speak to you on some pressing issues that I have and I need your assistance!"

"My friend, please tell me, how can I help you?"

Damu suddenly becomes angered listening to Lopez and his bullshit. "Look you piece of shit bottom feeder, you have been taking our money for a long time and you know what you were supposed to do as far as warning us or alerting us to this Federal shake down and you did nothing. You know that puts you in a very awkward position with me, Lopez."

"Damu, listen! There was nothing that I could do! The feds kept it so top secret, they didn't even tell me! But I did make sure that your name wasn't on the top thirty gangster list."

"And you think that helped me, Lopez? By not giving me any advance knowledge on the list and me not being able to warn anyone, I have all the Blood leadership in LA thinking that I am cooperating with law enforcement because I am not on that list. I am the only westside Blood leader not on the list, but that is neither here nor there. Now Lopez, I need you to help me with a few things immediately. The first thing that I need you to do is to get Brazyiak off that top thirty gangster list!"

"Look Damu..."

"Look shit, Lopez. I have a lot of dirt on you that covers various things and I will bring your ass down on Stones if you do not help me." The calm venom in Damu's voice is frightening.

"Okay, okay! Damu, let's calm down first and not do anything irrational. I have to look into some things. Let me see what I can do for you about Brazyiak."

"There isn't anything to see. You need to work something, Lopez!"

"Damu, I do have an issue that maybe we can work something out on. You do this for me and I will work on the Brazyiak situation for you."

"Go ahead. I'm listening."

"I need two favors for your one big one, Damu."

"I'm all ears. Keep going, Lopez."

"I need somebody X'd out, and I need this done with no traces."

"Who?"

Lopez hesitates for a moment. "It's a rich Latin businessman in the Valley. And the second part goes into helping Brazyiak get out of his situation. It would involve him testifying against a cop before a Federal Grand Jury for the prosecution. Are you familiar with an officer they call Eat 'em Up on the streets from Robbery Homicide?"

"Yeah, what criminal on the west side hasn't heard or encountered that dirty Nazi?"

"Well, that dirty Nazi has been under investigation by the FBI and LAPD Internal Affairs for quite some time now. If you wack who I want wacked, then I will ensure Brazyiak will be able to turn himself into the Feds under the guise of his cooperation in testimony against Eat 'em Up and I can almost guarantee he will walk away jail free, that's how bad they want to take this guy down."

Damu quickly analyzes the situation and says, "This is what I'm going to do Lopez. I have to talk to Brazyiak at length and see what he says about all of this since it involves his jacket with testimony. If he says it's going down, then I will arrange the hitters for the mission, but I'm not playing around on this, Lopez. If everything does not go down exactly as we discussed today on the phone, then my last act on Earth will be killing you, do you understand me? You hear me, Lopez?"

"Damu, c'mon, man! It's me; there is no need for threats and I definitely hear you loud and clear. Everything is understood, my friend. I know full well what you are capable of. I will be awaiting your call, Damu."

And just like that, they have a possible end to their life on the run.

"Brazyiak, I need to talk to you, Blood."

"Yeah, I was ear hustlin' while you was talkin' to Lopez and it seems like he got an out for us. Am I right, big homie?"

Damu breaks it down. "Most definitely, but as with most things involving politics there is a lot of shit attached to it."

"Shit like what, Blood?"

"Shit like you having a testimony on your jacket."

Brazyiak's face scrunches up as soon as Damu said testimony. "Blood, you want me to snitch on some niggas? Damu, you, outta all niggas, gotta know the YG don't get down like that, Blood! I ain't no muthafuckin' snitch!"

"I'm not asking you to snitch on any Gs, Blood. It's all about setting up that dirty pork chop Eat 'em up."

"Whoa. What? That wild ass pig from Robbery Homicide?"

"Exactly!"

"He shot my lil homie in the back, crippled his legs, and sent him up for ten in Pelican Bay in the SHU! Hell yeah, Blood! I'll do it to that pig! Do I get to smoke 'em, too?"

"Not right now, Blood, but the other part of the deal is murking someone."

"If not the pig ,who is it then?"

"Not sure who he is. Some rich dude from the Valley."

"On Dub S GB's; let's make that shit happen, Blood!" Brazyiak cracks a smile.

Damu divulges his escape plan for them. "I also have a plan to ensure that Lopez does not try to weasel out or try to play us in any way, Blood."

"Yeah, I knew you had somethin' up yo' sleeve. I know how you do it, homie."

Damu looks Brazyiak in the eyes. "But you are not going to like it since it involves the Crabs downstairs."

"Blood, what is you talkin' 'bout? What kind of plan is that? Me and that nigga J Loc been tryin' to kill each other since Wadsworth Elementary on the eastside! It ain't never gon' be right 'til I smoke that dude, Blood! You know how many time that Crab done tried to murk me? That nigga done sent a buncha homies restin'! Fuck that, Blood, I can't do nothin' wit' that nigga. I'd rather die!" But he sees that Damu is dead serious about them working together. "I guess I'm dying here tonight, Blood. That ain't goin' down."

Damu goes into rest assuring leader mode. "Brazyiak, I love you like the little brother I never had so you know I would never tell you to do something I would not do myself. I'm closer to you than my own brother Supreme. We have never let each other down homie and we never will. Why would I do anything to bring you harm, B? Trust me, Blood, what I have up my sleeve will get rid of that Crab J Loc and his whole set and get us where we need to be at! As a matter of fact, I am going to plan this out so good that our enemies will kill each other and all we have to do is sit back and watch, Blood!"

Once again, Damu's words of reason have calmed down Brazyiak.

"Blood, you ain't never let me down and you always have helped me and my hood, so I'm down for it." They both embrace and throw up the B. "I put my life in your hands homie!"

And with that, the chain of events are set into motion to change how street life will be lived in Los Angeles for years to come.

Damu checks outside the window one more time before grabbing his heat and heading downstairs to the apartment where the Crabs are lying in wait.

Damu selects two of the little homies from the Avenues to go downstairs. Bringing Brazyiak would just be asking for it; there is just too much animosity between him and J Loc, but Brazyiak is posted like Malcolm X in the window.

If these Crabs open fire or make any type of aggressive movements, then Brazyiak is dumping. Damu takes a deep breath, put his gun in his waistband, and looks Brazyiak square in the eyes. He gives him the mission look, one they have shared on too many occasions to list. He knows to shoot to kill if he feels anything funny.

Damu calmly closes the front door of the apartment behind him and walks slowly down the stairs to where the Crips are.

"Cuz, here come that Slob nigga Damu and a couple of youngsters with him!"

"They headin' right over here! Everybody load up and get in position!"

The front room of the small apartment is filled with about six Crips, all armored and ready to shoot. They move into formation under the instruction of J Loc.

"I know y'all niggas don't get a lot of action over there in the this part of town, but Imma ride out vet. Just fall in behind me and if any of these Slob niggas makes the slightest wrong move, shoot!" The Ethiopian Crips look a little shook but try to look hard.

This is what he has been waiting for, confrontation. He has waited long enough, too long if you ask him. Too much thinking is involved in waiting. He is ready to make a move whether good or bad; he is ready to loc! The part of his brain that was warning him that it's crazy to get into it with his enemies while the city is totally over run with feds has shut off.

He is a Crip. Loccing out is what he does to survive. He is ready to press the line and take things to the next level. That's his comfort zone and the only way he feels safe.

As Damu approaches the front door before he can

even knock, J Loc swings the door open with two pistols drawn, one in each hand.

"What the fuck wrong with you Slobs? On M Dubs, I'm giving you trey seconds to move or I'm smokin' you!"

"J Loc, relax and be easy."

"Fuck being easy Slob! I don't be shit! This straight Crippin' and I'm tired of layin' low, if this is how I'm gonna die, then fuck it, Cuz, then that's what it is!"

Damu knows that he has only a few seconds left to respond or his life and his plan of escape are over. He is already nervous that him and the little homies are drawing way to much attention standing in front of the Crips' door.

"Listen J Loc, smoke me, go ahead and do what you are going to do, but I came down here to offer you a way off the wanted list and a chance to get out of here safely. Let us in so we can talk about this like G's."

J Loc knows having these fools in front of their door for another minute is likely to bring out the heat with this crazy federal takeover, so he lets them in the small apartment. After some very awkward looks exchanged. J Loc speaks first.

"What the fuck you mean offer me somethin', nigga? I'm the nigga with two barrels aimed on yo' chest! Seems to me that I'm the deal maka, Cuz!"

"Yeah, you right about that, J Loc, but if I did not have to deal with you on business, then why else would I come down here without my gun out if I was not trying to talk to you about something?"

"I don't know, Cuz, to play them Slob ass mind games you Slobs do!"

Tension is starting to rise again.

Brazyiak is trying to keep an eye on what's happening and is ready to start shooting at the first signs of any trouble.

Damu tries to set a cooler mood and tells the lil homies to bring out some of that fire to smoke. The young Bloods whip out the blunts and light several for rotation. The Ethiopian Crips are eager to smoke and quickly let down their guard; J Loc isn't so easily swayed. Damu speaks to him.

"Man, we have been through this before earlier, J Loc. I have something that we both can benefit from, but I need you to hear me out!"

With both guns aimed at Damu's chest J Loc loudly barks, "Nigga, speak! I ain't stopped you from talking yet!"

Damu calmly continues. "I have some work that I think you may be interested in. It involves setting up Eat 'em Up."

As soon as Damu mentions Eat 'em Up, J Loc's facial expression changes from menacing to intrigued. He has been wanting to kill Eat 'em Up forever. He has made J Loc's life a living hell at every opportunity that he could.

"I'm listening, nigga. Continue." J Loc puts his guns down by his side.

Damu knows now that he has just bought some time to explain his plans without immediate danger from J Loc and the Crips. He looks up quickly towards the apartment window upstairs to let Brazyiak know not to do anything crazy right now.

"I have info that there is a Federal indictment on Eat 'em Up as well as an Internal Affairs investigation on him. The FBI wants him bad, even more than any of us, because they feel they have broken our hoods up and have us on the run. Now they really want his crooked ass bad! Word on the street is that you have been trying to kill each other for a minute. Now, I have a homie that's going to put Eat 'em Up away forever through his testimony, but if we start a shoot out and kill each other, then I do not get out of here to contact the homie and you don't get this cracker off your back! All I'm asking you to do is let me leave the apartments with no gunplay and let my homie stay up stairs safe until I return."

"Fuck that. Y'all niggas running game, Cuz. You tryin' to go get some mo' Slobs and come back here and get at us. And why would I ever help Slobs especially that bitch ass nigga Brazyiak? Me and that nigga been beefin' our whole lives, Cuz."

Damu is in his mind control zone and throws a bit of reverse psychology at J Loc. "I came down here trying to save my freedom and live, but if you want to kill me do it, but you are going to have to shoot me in my back because I am walking through this courtyard and putting the plan in motion to set Eat 'em Up's ass up!" He looks at the lil Bloods. "Lil Bloods, we out." The young Avenues jump up and quickly leave the apartment.

Damu looks at J Loc and then turns his back from J Loc and the Crip apartment and heads to the center of the courtyard heading towards the exit. His heart is beating faster than it ever has in his life as he walks. He reasons J Loc will not shoot him in the back because he follows gangster rules and knows how real Gs frown on shooting someone from the back. He also knows that they are all scared of bringing the heat into their little hideout.

He also knows J Loc wants the glory of killing him, but not like this. He is gambling his life on J Loc adhering to the gangster code. As he continues to walk toward the exit and out the gates without a hole in his back, his gamble has paid off.

Brazyiak watches as Damu leaves the complex and thinks for one brief moment that he should just start shooting at the Crips and end his life on his own terms. But that thought leaves as quickly as it entered and he stays in position in the window waiting for Damu to return.

Damu calls Lopez. "Lopez, it's Damu."

"Damu, good to hear from you, buddy."

"Cut the short talk, man. I have done what I need to do on my end and my part of the plan is in motion."

"Great. Now I need to give you the instructions on where, when, and the particulars of everything."

"Yeah, okay."

"I'll call you tomorrow and give the next round of info and you can take it from there, Damu."

Damu cuts the call off and puts the cell phone back

in his pocket and slips behind a building to think for a moment.

He has been reviewing and revising his plan to deal with the Crips and Lopez over and over again in his mind. He knows that one false move blows everything that he has worked for since he came home from YA. He closes both his eyes and asks Allah to guide him through this ordeal.

He quickly opens his eyes and says Allah Hu Akbar. He is absolutely sure of what he has to do now and confidently walks back to the hideout.

Inside the hideout, he pulls back the shades and takes a look towards the apartment with J Loc and the Crips. As if on cue, someone pulls one of the curtains back and reveals an AK 47, showing Damu that they are watching him as well.

Brazyiak is getting restless "Damu! Blood, I been on edge up here posted on these Crabs!"

"My G, Blood, I appreciate everything you have ever done for me, homie. That's why we are even doing what we are doing now, so that you can have a new start, Brazyiak! I talked to Lopez and everything is set in motion. He is going to call me tomorrow with the rest of the information on the hit and then we will plan our part of it from there."

"Aight, Blood. You know killin' is the best part for me. Just get the details and I'm ready to put the work in. Bein' around these Crabs and not bein' able to murk 'em got me ready to let off!"

"That's what's up, Blood. Now there is a twist to the

plot though, homie. I spent the last two hours thinking how we can kill two birds with one stone, meaning, how do we get rid of Lopez and these Crabs at the same time, especially J Loc's ass!"

"What did you come up with, big homie?"

"We are taking J Loc with us on the mission."

Brazyiak can't believe what he is hearing. "Look Blood, it was enough just going through what we just went through wit' them Crabs earlier. Blood, on my Momma, I'm gon' kill that Crab J Loc at the first chance I get. I can't be nowhere close to him with a gun and not shoot him in his face at least, Blood! Real talk, Damu, it took everything I had inside me not to kill them niggas earlier."

"Brazyiak, homie, just fall in line with me, Blood. I promise the twist I have for our enemies will go down in the pages of street history!"

Brazyiak knows he really has no choice at this point, but to follow Damu's plan. "Fuck it Blood, let's make history then!"

16

MONTEBELLO MISSION AKA FUCK THE MOB!

Damu peers out of the window of the apartment. Thoughts move rapidly through his head as he contemplates his next move. He stops processing his thoughts to ponder on his current condition.

I am so fucking tired of walking these steps to go downstairs to talk to these Crabs, but it's what I have to do in order to keep everything in motion for my plan to work. I hate having to listen to all their Crab posturing and machismo from a bunch of bastards that I really want to shoot on sight, but I cannot.

But repressing emotions and following through on strategy is what makes a great leader that is what I have to remember.

Damu descends down the staircase to the apartment holding the Crips and knocks. Once again, he is putting his self in the line of fire while his trusted young killer Brazyiak holds position in the window upstairs with an AK in hand.

The door opens to the apartment and Damu speaks, "J Loc, I need to speak to you one-on-one homie!

J Loc is standing with one hand on his pistol and holding a smoking blunt in the other. He twists his face into a full gangster scrawl. "Whad up, Loco? Come inside so none of these squares start tripping and calls the ones."

Damu steps into the apartment and closes the door behind him. "First off, J Loc, I wanted to say I appreciate you for keeping it gangster on letting me leave out of here unharmed and being able to put the red light in motion to get everything done concerning Eat 'em Up."

J Loc exhales his smoke in Damu's face and says, "That's just how us Mid City Rip Ridas do, Cuz." J Loc inches in closer to Damu to the point where both their noses are almost touching and says, "I'm gon' keep it all the way Crip, Damu. Everything is cool right now until we can get at y'all niggas all the way official in these streets. Ain't nobody tryin' to tangle wit' dem Feds right now. But don't get it fucked up, Damu, 'cuz as soon as this shit is ova, I'm on your homeboy head, and me and you still got bidness to take care of on the gang!"

Looking directly into J Loc's eyes, Damu says, "I couldn't agree with you more homie. We will get a chance to air out all our grievances real soon, but right now, I have a proposition for you."

J Loc looks puzzled. "What you talkin' bout, mane? You breathin' right now and bein' able to walk outta here to handle ya thang, Cuz, is becuz I let you. It ain't shit we need to discuss now, but when Eat 'em Up ass get arrested and when I get some of this fuckin' heat offa me on these streets Cuz..."

"Come on, J Loc. Do not front for me, nigga. You

have been on the run laying low and haven't been able to move the way you want to or get money the way you want to, just like us, and I have a remedy to both of those things for you, if you hear me out."

Still posturing and holding the gun, J Loc says, "Look nigga, you don't know shit about my pockets and I move how the fuck I wanna move, Feds or not. But go 'head, continue wit' what you was about to say on whatever, Cuz!" But J Loc puts his gun away.

Damu knows now that he has piqued J Loc's interest. He has his full attention and he is about to use this moment to drag him further into his intricate plot. "I have a possible situation arranged that I could use your expertise and involvement in. It is for five thousand dollars and an opportunity to get the fuck out of this hideout for a minute." Damu pauses, then continues. "And I know all this hiding out is getting to you and you want to move. I'm saying, come on, J Loc, before the injunctions came out, you were all on the news with that rap guy Strapz. You are probably the most famous young Crip in LA right now."

"Ain't no probably, Cuz. I am. TMZ, the paparazzi, and all them niggas know the Loc!"

Damu nods. "And that's why your ass is over here hiding just like Brazyiak and me. We all are too high profile to be anywhere hot. I cannot contact any of my homies to do this job for me because their lines are tapped by the Feds, but I have to complete this thing in order to ensure that the arrangement with Eat 'em Up goes down and that is why I need your help."

"Cuz, you right. After Strapz got smoked at the Beverly Center and the Feds hit the hood, I been on the run. That's real talk, Cuz. I could use them five raccs and I'm antsy as hell to shoot a nigga since I didn't get to let off on y'all two niggas!" J Loc smiles an evil smile.

"Well, it is on the table and the move is on you. But I need an answer by the morning so I can get our ride situation set up and get the bread ready for after the mission, so you have to let me know by then."

"Nigga, it's a wrap! Set it up! I gotta get outta here and I need that bread, too."

"Aight, I will put everything in motion to move in the morning and by tomorrow night, we should be ready to ride. You will get the money right after the mission is complete."

"So I'm bringing the K and the AR. Do we need more for the mission?"

"No, that should be good. That's heavy artillery right there," says Damu. "And one more thing: wear the squarest clothes possible. I don't want us getting spotted by the feds when we leave these apartments." Damu stands up.

"I gotchu," says J Loc.

"And by the way, it's not me and you. It's you and Brazyiak."

As soon as he says that, Damu heads to the door, looking back for just a moment.

J Loc is frozen. The combination of what he had last heard, the blunt he has been pulling on, and the realization that he is about to go on a mission with his worst enemy has left him speechless and stuck. His body language or lack thereof is enough to tell Damu he has struck a chord and he has J Loc in a position right where he wants him.

Now Damu is the one smiling as he walks up the stairs.

The chess game has begun.

———————————————————————

The next morning...

Damu has called Lopez and arranged for a courier service van to be dropped off by the coffee shop two doors down from the Carl's Jr in Little Ethiopia.

Inside the van are a box of surgical gloves, two courier delivery uniforms, ski masks, two sets of work gloves, an address to the hit, and a GPS.

Each killer individually prepares to do his work in a different manner; it is a ritual that both gangsters go into before they murder.

For Brazyiak, preparation entails listening to hip-hop, usually some Tupac, and bumping it as loud as possible. For J Loc, he loses himself in a meditation-like trance, concentrating on his breathing and blocking out everything else.

After both have completed their rituals, they finish getting ready while Damu gives Brazyiak a bag with some clothes and the final instructions. "Here. Wear this polo shirt and these jeans. It would be terrible if the ones clipped us on the way to the van."

"Damn, homie! You got me dressing like a cornball!"

"Brazyiak, homie, this is the most important mission of our lives, don't trip on that small shit," Damu says. "I want you to drive the courier van. The address and GPS navigation are ready for you. You are going to Montebello, up in the hills. Blood, if anything in the slightest looks strange, call my jack."

"Yeah, I gotcha, Damu, and if the Crab does anything outta pocket, I'm smokin' him, Blood!"

"Understood."

Brazyiak grabs the AK near the front window of the apartment and wraps it inside a jacket and heads downstairs toward the van.

J Loc grabs the AR and his AK and wraps both of them in a bed sheet and moves towards the front door. He takes one long look around the room. These are not his riders from his hood, but rather gangbang homies. There is no need for an exchange of pleasantries or a need of reassurance.

If he survives the mission, he will see them again. If he does not survive the mission, he is also good with that outcome. He throws the Crip C up in the air and moves with the guns out the door.

J Loc and Brazyiak both meet up at the courier van at the same time.

At first there is very little eye-to-eye contact between them and no conversation at all. Brazyiak moves from the front of the van to the driver side. J Loc steps to the passenger side. As they enter the vehicle both do a careful inspection of their respective sides. They both grab a courier uniform and gloves and change their clothes.

After switching clothes and getting gloved up, they both unwrap their weapons and position them for access and concealment in case of a run in with law enforcement.

They are both ready to kill.

Brazyiak checks the address and sets them in the GPS.

Driving from Little Ethiopia in Mid City to Montebello, which is past East LA and on the way to the Inland Empire, at this time of day will take about 45 minutes on the 10 freeway.

In the streets of Los Angeles, anything can happen at any time depending on chance and circumstance. Murder can be accidental, spontaneous, or planned.

J Loc and Brazyiak are products of that murderous mentality. They have both had to kill in order to survive. They have also had to kill under orders when they fully didn't understand the meaning behind the killing, but that's what riders do, kill on instruction with no questions asked.

Today is one of those missions that they don't fully understand the reasoning behind it; they just know what they have to do. Circumstance has two lifelong enemies working together. Just two days ago, they were seconds away from shooting one another.

This is the nature of the beast that is gang-banging in the streets of LA. Shit happens the way it happens, and sometimes even the worst of enemies can be aligned for a common cause.

They ride in silence until J Loc decides to break the silence and asks Brazyiak some questions about past hood incidents. Even through the hatred, there is a level of mutual respect, and in this situation that has forced them together, they both have a lot of curiosity about the other and the two slowly start to talk.

They are approaching their exit on the 10 for Montebello, and it is about to go down. Brazyiak maneuvers the courier van off the 10 at the designated exit and they move in local traffic to the direction of the hills of Montebello. Brazyiak checks the GPS and texts Damu to let him know they are in Montebello and that everything is running according to plan.

Two hated enemies sit right next to each other and are minutes away from killing someone, even though they are now speaking and everything seems cool, this moment is not lost on either one.

Brazyiak thinks to himself while driving, "I don't want to do anythin' to jeopardize tha mission, but I can't get over that I'm this close to this Crab and can't kill'um!"

J Loc looks outside his passenger window, saying to himself in thought, "If this Slob does anythin' I don't like, I'm dumpin' on his bitch ass, fuck everything!"

The van gets closer to their intended target and they start their elevation into the hills. They continue moving upwards into the hills for about a quarter mile and pull into a gated community.

Brazyiak leans over from inside the courier van and speaks into the security gate voice box, "We have a delivery for Mr. Lopez."

A voice speaks back telling them to turn into the security office when the gate opens. Brazyiak and J Loc look at each other and confirm through their eye contact they are both ready to kill at any attempt made by anyone to stop them of achieving their goal.

The gate opens and the van pulls up to the security office. A small balding overweight Mexican man approaches the van with a sheet of paper in his hand. "Hey guys. Just take a right as you leave the main driveway and follow these directions. Mr. Lopez is home and should answer the door."

"Thanks and have a good day." Brazyiak grabs the directions and heads right off the first drive. They pull up to the house and both killers immediately grab their concealed weapons. There is no trust of each other or in the situation they are involved in, so any discrepancies today will be met with gunplay.

"Blood, is you ready? I'm goin' to tha door, grab that box and follow me."

Brazyiak hops out of the van with guns in both sides of his waistband and a fake invoice in hand. He moves stealth-like, with a confidence and bop that a killer acquires from years of attacking his prey. He rings the doorbell. A tall buff Mexican man with no shirt and covered in tattoos answers the door. He looks nothing like Brazyiak imagined him.

"I have a delivery here for Mr. Lopez. Are you Mr. Lopez, sir?"

"Yeah, I'm Lopez."

As soon as he reaches for the paperwork, Lopez knows that something is wrong. His gangster sense is warning him and he responds to it. He starts to pull back as Brazyiak pulls the gun in the front of his waistband and shoves it into Lopez's chest.

On cue, J Loc removes his AR out of the empty delivery box. Lopez pushes Brazyiak and turns to make a break into the foyer of his home, running for his life. Brazyiak and J Loc waste no time following him. He is prey and he must die, but shooting him from the front porch will bring on to much attention. As bullets move from Brazyiak's silencer-equipped gun, it's obvious who will be dying today.

"Fuck you, beana! On Westside, Gangsta Bloods rot in hell, you hat dancing muthafucka!"

Lopez falls from the close range shots and collapses midway on the staircase.

J Loc goes into action and starts pistol whipping and stomping whatever little bit of life is left in Lopez out of his body.

Both J Loc and Brazyiak have been raised to hate Mexicans. They transfer this hate onto this man they do not know. They hate him because he represents the LA they hate and have to survive in every day. In less than two minutes Lopez is a bloody corpse as both men kick, stomp, spit, and pistol-whip the life out of him.

"Cuz, I'm goin' to the van to get our change of clothes. Keep an eye out and see if anybody heard or saw anythin'."

Brazyiak moves down the stairs towards the front door.

J Loc knows this is his chance to kill Brazyiak. It is a one-shot kill, and he will just tell Damu the Mexican shot Brazyiak as they struggled to kill him. But in that one moment, J Loc hesitates and Brazyiak makes it to the van. J Loc will have another day to try to kill Brazyiak, but today is not that day.

Brazyiak quickly returns from the van and throws J Loc a replacement uniform to change into. "Homie, go and check tha rooms upstairs, and see what valuables this Ese has up in here." Brazyiak then throws J Loc a large duffle bag. "I'm gon' check the bottom part of the house!"

J Loc grabs the clothes and says, "Yeah Cuz, I got you I'll be back in trey minutes."

Both killers spring into action. But as Brazyiak moves down the stairs again he notices something on the wall of the staircase.

"Cuz, that's Councilman Lopez and this fool hugged up in one them pictures. Look!"

Brazyiak takes note of what he just saw and moves in the foyer area. He removes his bloody uniform with his surgical gloves and looks up to the nearest wall to hold on to as he catches his balance.

Brazyiak also notices a pic that looks straight out of

prison with the guy he just shot and a bunch of what look like head honchos in the Mexican Mafia.

Brazyiak gets a fucked up feeling in his stomach. The kind that usually arrives right before bad news arrives. He keeps looking at the wall in the living room and sees pictures of Councilman Lopez and the dude they just murdered.

There are pictures of them as babies, as little kids, and as grown men together. This is too much, he has to call Damu, but only after they get out of the gated community safely. "Cuz, what the hell? This nigga Lopez is Councilman Lopez's brother?"

J Loc comes down the steps. "Cuz, what's crackin'?"

"Homie, I think we just murked a member of the Mexican mafia!"

J Loc looks at the prison picture and starts tripping. "Oh shit, Cuz! I thought we were murking some rich businessman, not a Mexican mafia leader. That shit would cost a lot more then five racks!"

Brazyiak opens the empty fake delivery box. "Look man, give me your bloody clothes for this box. I don't know what the fuck is goin' on wit' all this shit nigga, but we need to get out of here and figure it out."

J Loc throws his bloody uniform into the empty box Brazyiak is holding. Brazyiak puts his clothes in the same box, closes the top, and puts both straps back into his waistband. He grabs the box and his duffle bag and puts them in the back of the van and J Loc throws his duffle bag in and closes the door. They both jump in position in the van and head to the security office. The fat balding security guard opens the gate to let them out.

"Have a nice day."

Brazyiak smiles back at the guard. "Have a good one, too!"

Brazyiak drives the van downward from the Hills and calls Damu. "Damu, Blood! We smoked the Ese and we headin' back home, but some wild shit went down, Blood!"

Damu is taken aback. "What do you mean? Did someone see or hear anything?"

"Naw, naw, nothing like that, Blood. It's the Ese who we smoked. Did you know who that muthafucka was, Blood?"

"It was some rich businessman, right?"

"Naw, Blood! That fool looks to be a high ranking member of the Mexican mafia and Councilman Lopez's brotha!"

"What the fuck?"

"Yeah, yeah! He was covered in tats and had prison yard flicks in his crib along with all kinda flicks of him and Councilman Lopez together since they were kids until recently. Blood, I think Lopez put us in a big fuckin' twist!"

"You maybe right, homie, but right now I want you to concentrate on getting back here safely. Everything good with you and the Crab, though?"

"Yeah, we all flame! Dude did his work and we headed back to the spot. Imma call you when I get off the 10."

"Over and out, Blood."

17

TESTIMONY, POLITICIANS, AND FREEDOM

Brazyiak calls Damu to inform him of his location. "Blood, we droppin' off the van at San Vicente and Olympic. We should be at the apartments in fifteen minutes!"

"Okay, I will be standing at the gate to let you in"

Brazyiak and J Loc are moving through the cover of nightfall through the massive Los Angeles freeway system back to Little Ethiopia to their perspective hide outs. Surprisingly, the animosity between the two has for the moment cooled off. They discard of the van at the drop-off spot and walk back to their apartment hideout where Damu greets them both at the entrance.

"Good to see you both made it back here without any problems. J Loc, here you go," Damu slides J Loc a paper bag with $5,000 in it. "I appreciate everything that you have done. You are a man of your word."

J Loc's tries not to look to happy to receive the cash from his sworn enemies and all three of them move quickly, so as not to bring any unwanted attention from neighbors and other eyes.

"Brazyiak, don't think its ova, nigga! You know what Imma need from you, Cuz, on M Dub Gangstas!"

Brazyiak answers back. "Cuz, you can get it any day! Ain't nothin' changed!"

The two exchange mad dog glances that somehow don't have the same bite as they did before and they each go to their respective apartments.

Inside the apartment that Damu and Brazyiak have been sharing, Brazyiak opens up about all the confusion and anger he has been holding inside him.

"Blood! All this shit that has happened to me in the last few has me fucked up, Damu! The federal take-over, wackin' tha beana wit' that Crab J Loc, testifyin' on this pig Eat 'em Up. This shit is breakin' me down, Blood!"

"Brazyiak, this has been the most difficult time in my life besides going to jail. What I learned from my incarceration and that period of darkness made me the person you respect today, Blood. You are the strongest solider that I have ever encountered in my life. I would lie my life down for you in a moment's notice. Allah is testing us to see how resilient we are in times of need. This is all a part of the creator's plan!"

"Yeah, I know. What don't kill you makes you stronga ,and I ain't neva been one to trip offa livin' or dyin', Blood. It's just that eva since I came back from Tennessee, I been lookin' at my life a lil different than I eva have before. When I was out there wit' my auntie and Shannon, it was the first time since I was a lil kid that I felt like a part of a family, Blood. I been killin' and shootin' for so long, Blood, that I ain't neva sat down and thought about why I even do the shit that I do! This whole time we been on the run has forced a nigga to look at my life and how fucked up it has been! I don't know what's gon' happen wit' this testimony shit, but I do know that thangs ain't neva gon' be like they was befo' all this fed shit. I ain't neva gon' stop bein' a G, but I am finna get my shit togetha, Blood!"

Damu smiles at Brazyiak. "Blood, you are growing up and accepting responsibility for your actions. I am glad to hear a lot of those things coming from you! We all have to grow and evolve, and in that growth, there is always a period of uncertainty moving from the old you into the new you, and that is where you are right now. You helped me build the Blood Alliance, and once we are able to move past these legal issues, Blood, we will rule LA as we are supposed to!"

"I gotchu, Blood! You know I always gotta get that reassurance from my big brotha!" They both exchange the Blood handshake. "Speakin' of brothas, Blood, I got a muthafuckin' brotha out here! My auntie told me Big Brazy got anotha bitch pregnant while my moms was pregnant!"

"Welcome to the half-brother club, homie! You are now about to see what me and that nigga Supreme have been dealing with for our entire lives!"

"You probably right on that, too, since the nigga more than likely is a Crab! His momma was a Crab on the east-side!"

"Are you serious Blood? You know what is really brazy, Blood? You may have killed your own brother in the streets and not have even known!"

"You right, Blood, but fuck it! Crabs gotta get cracked!"

They both laugh.

———————————————————————

Meanwhile, in his hideout, J Loc reunites with the Ethiopian Crips.

"Cuz, welcome back! The homies was worried about you, out there running with the enemies!"

All the Crips in the room focus on J Loc as he walks into the apartment. "You gotdamn right I'm back, Cuz! What? Y'all thought some Slobs was gon' knock me off? Y'all niggas is trippin'. It don't matter if I'm tha last one left on the streets. It's still gangstas movin'!"

Although he appears to be confident and brave, J Loc is posturing for his Crip allies because for the first time ever in his life he is actually scared. He just killed a member of the Mexican mafia, and even for him, this is way over his head, not to mention that the last few months he has been through a whirlwind of murder, shootings, fleeing law enforcemen,t and the death and destruction of most of his gang. His closest homie Lover Boy and that rapper Strapz were killed in broad daylight in front of him at the Westside mall and that prompted the federal takeover and gang injunctions on the westside of Los Angeles. Big Bo Peep, the only father figure in his life, was murdered and he was forced to send his son Lil Bo Peep into exile after he killed his homie Blue Demon in a botched robbery.

Then, after he left Los Angeles to avoid law enforcement, he got caught up in the most infamous gang shooting in YouTube history when he shot six Crips at a Strapz concert in Pittsburgh and it became plastered all over the internet. He has also been fighting a war with that crooked LAPD Robbery Homicide detective Eat 'em Up who has been trying to tie him to Blue Demon's murder and to the shootings in Pittsburgh. He is frayed and worn out and all he has left is his gangsta persona.

J Loc goes into his stash in the apartment and pulls out some medical marijuana and a blunt. He rolls the weed without saying a word to anyone in the room and lights it up. As he becomes high and hazy from the blunt, he accepts that his life of 19 short years on the earth meant nothing to anyone. Pulling the blunt and exhaling the smoke, he decides to die in a hail of gunfire. He will gangsta Crip it until the end.

The next morning upstairs, Damu and Brazyiak eat breakfast and watch TV.

"Blood, today is the day, Damu!"

"Yes, today is that day, Brazyiak. Are you ready?"

"I guess I'm 'bout as ready as I will eva be to work wit' da Feds and testify on this nigga Eat 'em Up, Blood!"

"I know you are worried about having a smear on your jacket from the testimony, but my lawyer has assured me that as long as the Feds play according to the rules then your testimony will be sealed and hidden. You will have nothing to worry about as long as you do not come into the Federal court system."

"I ain't trippin' on that shit, Blood! That's all niggas do is snitch now anyway! How niggas gon' come at me when they flippin' on they own homies? I just don't like fuckin' wit' tha police! These niggas is always on some backhand shit! That say one thang and do anotha type shit!"

"I agree with you on the snake nature of a cop but you have to understand how to handle a snake. You never put your hands in the snake pit and you will never get bitten! I have a few tricks up my sleeve to ensure that you get the best treatment possible."

"Like what Blood?"

Damu flashes a large and sinister grin and says, "Remember when I told you I had a way to get rid of J Loc and Councilman Lopez?"

"Yeah, I rememba Blood!"

"I still have that plan in motion. What if I told you I have Lopez on tape talking about his participation in bribery payoffs, murder for hires, and other crimes?"

"I would say that sounds like some ole Damu brainiac shit, Blood!"

"What if I could also tell you that I have Lopez on tape recordings with leaders and members of several recognized gangs that are on the Top Thirty Most Wanted List?"

"Blood, I would have to hug yo' smart ass and say Soo Whoop! Blood, you got me covered!"

"Brazyiak, you are beyond being covered, Blood!

These things insure you will be treated fairly and just, and if Lopez tries to wiggle out of anything, we will serve him on a platter to the Feds!"

Brazyiak is moving all around the apartment with energy. He grabs his gun and points it at the front window. "Blood, what you just told me makes me feel good as hell! Maybe I can't kill that bitch ass nigga J Loc, but to know he is goin' down makes my day! Shit, I am ready to meet the Feds now! Let's be out, Blood!"

Meanwhile, downstairs, J Loc is severely depressed. The only thing that comforts his worries is thinking about Carla back in Champaign. She has been texting him throughout the Federal takeover, but he hasn't answered her yet. He can't focus on his survival day to day and try to be a good boyfriend, too. But for the first time in his life, J Loc is thinking beyond the Mid City Westside Gangsta Crips. The takeover has decimated the only family he has ever known in his life. He has watched on TV as law enforcement destroyed and arrested his neighborhood and homies.

He hasn't been able to check on his grandmother in weeks. It has finally hit him that he is all on his own. The thought of a life after jail is starting to sound better than no life at all. J Loc has started thinking about giving himself up. He had always pictured himself dying in a hail of gunfire. It was his romanticized version of going all out. But it is becoming clearer with each passing day that he can survive, it doesn't have to be that way. J Loc is finally dealing with being Jason and the thoughts of a life after banging.

———————————————————————

Damu and Brazyiak arrive at Councilman Lopez's headquarters with a lawyer in tow and prepare for Brazyiak to turn himself in to Federal authorities for testimony. Lopez is getting ready for a press conference to announce the joint task force and the arrest of Eat 'em Up. Damu takes Lopez to the side away from his advisors and staff to speak to him in private.

"Lopez, I have honored every part of our deal and I appreciate you creating an opportunity for Brazyiak to clear his name. I just want to make sure that we are clear on a few things."

"Okay, shoot, Damu. But be quick. I need to get ready for this press conference!"

"Lopez, I have some insurance to make sure that I do not have any problems from you on keeping your word to me. Here. I want you to listen to something."

Damu press play on his iPhone and throws it to Lopez. He hears himself on the recording talking and stops it. "Come on, Damu! What type of shit is this? I have done every fucking thing you have wanted me to do and now you hit me with taped conversations of me!"

"Lopez, you and I both know you are a scum bucket! You are always lying and you even had us to kill your own fucking brother, not to mention that he was in the Mexican Mob, which is a whole 'nother issue we will deal with after this is one! Needless to say, I do not trust you."

"Well, maybe you're right, Damu. Maybe I am a piece of shit. But that doesn't make you any fuckin' better than me! You kill people, too, asshole! But you do it for money and power! I killed my brother because he was sleeping with my wife! See Mr. Self-Righteous, I had my reasons. I was born a good kid. I was just like any other kid I knew until my brother came back from YA and started introducing me to all sorts of devilish shit! He was bigger and stronger than me used to punk me regularly and there was nothing I could do about it. So I kept all that anger inside to myself and said fuck everybody because nobody helped me! I lied, cheated, and stole to get to the top and I finally made it here. I was even able to get in a position to get payback on his ass back by fucking his daughter and taking that most precious thing from him." Lopez paused and looked out the window. "But life doesn't work how we plan, Damu, and my brother found out I was fucking my niece. He told my wife and she starting fucking him for revenge and then he began to extort me. First on his own behalf and then later for the Mexican Mafia. I couldn't take it anymore! Isn't it enough that he took my soul and now he wants everything that I worked for! So I came up with the scheme to kill him. Big shit! Look Damu, I don't have shit anymore, I am a shell of a man. You do what the fuck you think is right because honestly I don't know and don't give a fuck anymore."

Lopez strolls out of the room to go to the press conference. Damu says nothing. What could he say even if he could muster the words? He has just watched a man break down. He walks back into the room with his attorney and Brazyiak just as the Feds are ready to take Brazyiak.

"Blood, I'm finna be out! Your lawyer said I gotta be in general lockup with all the other gangs so niggas won't figure out I'm testifyin'!"

"Just do what has to be done and you will be released afterwards, Blood! Stay on your square and try to piece up the BA while you are locked down!"

"Sho' thang, Blood!"

Brazyiak is escorted out by the Feds into custody. Damu is sick at the sight of his best friend being carried away in cuffs, but he understands it must be done in order to clear his name.

18

Brothers? The Hell We Are!

Brazyiak is deep inside the Federal detention city in downtown Los Angeles in a processing holding cell. He is amazed at how vast and massive the facility is. This is his first time in his criminal career that he has been arrested and jailed in this facility. The Federal takeover has allowed the Federal agencies to arrest and hold any LA gang members without provocation and there are bangers everywhere. For obvious reasons, gang members are held and processed based on their gang allegiance. Brazyiak is brought to the Blood holding cell.

He automatically calls rank and goes into Brazyiak mode. "Blood up! Dub gang!"

Brazyiak's exclamation reverberates through the wall of the cell. Suddenly, about twenty members of the Westside Gangsta Bloods emerge, including Lil Mousey. "Brazyiak! Blood, it sho' is good to have you up in here, big homie. Shit is brazy in here! Niggas is goin' at each otha every day on some bullshit, Blood!"

"Is that right, Blood? Who been callin' shots for tha hood in here?"

"Yo, eastside homie Lil Bick Back. You know he

was already in here for a minute since he got cracked but he been trippin', Blood! He done split all us up on some eastside versus westside shit and he been sidin' them eastie niggas up wit' all kinda perks and leavin' us wit' nothin', Blood! He do for otha eastie gangs befo' he even fuck wit' our hood, Blood!"

"Don't even trip on none of that. I am finna set these niggas straight! We gotta get our hood togetha in here and unify as one. It is all bad outside. Niggas is stuck in this bitch for however and we need to be as strong as possible in here!"

"You know I am wit' you, big homie. Just let me know when you ready to ride out on these niggas!"

"Blood, I'm ready now! What's tha weapon situation like?"

"Tha Feds come thru every day sweepin' for knives! Niggas is in here catchin' fades like a muthafucka! PJ Bloods is in here servin' everybody since they got tha most niggas in here."

"I ain't trippin' on none of that shit, Blood! We gon' organize and ride out and if Lil Bick Back ain't wit' us, his ass is dead! You know I grew up with Blood on the east. He ain't no kinda hog, he just a hustla. I'm assertin' my position as second in charge of the Blood Alliance and shot calla for the Dub to shut that nigga down!"

Brazyiak quickly puts a plan in motion to confront Lil Bick Back and the Eastside faction of his neighborhood. He rallies the 20 gang members from his hood and he puts them up to speed on what he and Lil Mousey have discussed and prepares them for combat. Brazyiak is a fearless leader and excels at confrontation. He leads by brutal example only. His words are always backed up by his actions. He watches the guards and decides he will confront Lil Bick Back after the guards change shift.

Meanwhile back in little Ethiopia, J Loc is preparing to head back to his neighborhood. He has thought about it for several days and has decided to turn himself into the Federal authorities. Carla has been texting and calling him incessantly and he has finally started answering her calls and talking to her. She has told him that she will move to LA and take care of his grandmother while he is incarcerated and support him in anyway she can. For the first time in his life, J Loc is in love with something besides gangbanging. He has never pictured himself involved with a woman beyond being sexual partners, but he knew from the first time he saw Carla that he felt something that he had never experienced before. Her love has forced him to look at one thing he has always thrown to the wind, his future. Damu gave him five racks for his part in the murder for hire he did in Montebello, and he can leave that money to his grandmother to make sure that he has money on his books. All he has to do now is call Mr. Stein, Strapz's lawyer, and work out the procedure to turn himself in.

He nervously dials Mr. Stein and starts the call that will change his life. "Mr. Stein, this is J Loc, Strapz's homie.

Do you remembuh me?"

"J Loc, how in the hell could I forget you! I have one word for you, Pittsburgh, my dear friend! Are you on a secured line, buddy?"

"No, that doesn't matter, Mr. Stein. I know I was supposed to call you earlier but shit has been crazy for me out here since Strapz was killed."

"I know. I've been watching the news and I saw your face on the Top Thirty list."

"Yeah, that's part of the reason I am calling you. Between the Top Thirty thang and the shooting in Pittsburgh, I think I am finally ready to turn myself in, Mr. Stein."

"Okay. I can work something out with some Federal prosecutor friends I know for you to turn yourself in and work out the best possible deal for you."

"I appreciate that, Mr. Stein."

"Strapz really had a lot of love for you, J Loc! We would both talk about your escapades together and be in awe of how you live your life. You are like a black Billy the Kid, J Loc. You've been through an incredible amount of adversity and struggle in your life and you still continue to move forward as a true warrior We both admired that quality in you, man. That shooting you did in Pittsburgh, believe it or not, put Strapz back on the map and was starting to take his career in an entirely different direction! Because of the media attention to that shooting, Quentin Tarantino is dedicating his new movie in Strapz's honor. Now I think once this media hype dies down, I can work on getting some appeals on your behalf, but," Stein pauses. "I have to be honest. You are going to have to do some time."

"I know. I ain't trippin'. It's just life catchin' up wit' me fo' all tha shit I done did. Imma be ready to turn myself in around two days from now. I need to check in with my family and get my money situation together and I'm good!"

"I'll put everything in motion. You just call me when you are ready, J Loc, and stay out of trouble in the meantime, kid!"

J Loc gets off the phone and gathers his stuff from the apartment. At nightfall, he will be moving through the streets heading back to his beloved Mid City Westside Gangsta Crip neighborhood.

◼——————————————◼

Inside the massive Blood holding cell block, word has quickly spread that Brazyiak has been captured and is inside. Before Brazyiak, Lil Mousey, and his squad of Westside Gangsta Bloods can advance with their plan of assault, they are met in their section of the holding tank by a contingent of Blood leaders from all over the city including Lil Bick Back and OG Big Red from PJ Bloods.

Brazyiak stands defiantly in the front of this assembled group and says, "Soo Whoop! What is y'all niggas doin'? Givin' me a welcomin' comittee or somethin, Bloods?"

OG Big Red's massive arms surround Brazyiak and hug him. "YG, glad you still alive, Blood! Where da fuck is Damu at, Blood?"

Brazyiak senses the hostile tone in OG Big Red's question and pulls himself from his grasp. "Blood is out there tryin' to get tha biz straight! Y'all niggas left us there to die, Blood! Salted Bloods' name without no paperwork or nothin!"

"Blood! What you mean, paperwork? Niggas don't need no muthafuckin' evidence. Everybody locked up but dat nigga! What mo' need to be said? We all in here, and dat Blood ain't!"

"That's becuz Blood had a politician lookin' out for him on the payroll of the Blood Alliance. The same Blood Alliance that we gave y'all niggas guns and work wit' and y'all niggas abandoned as soon as shit got tough out here! Look here OG Big Red, I ain't finna get in to all that shit yet on tha Blood Alliance and how niggas didn't keep it g. I gots some shit I need to work out wit' this bitch ass nigga right here, Lil Bick Back!"

Brazyiak hits Lil Bick Back in the face knocking him to the ground. The two are separated as OG Big Red restrains Brazyiak.

Lil Bick Back raises his bloodied face off the ground. He stands up behind another gang member and yells, "Blood! What da fuck wrong wit' you?"

"Let me go, OG Big Red! This ain't got shit to do wit' PJ Bloods! This is all Gangsta Blood bizness!"

OG Big Red releases Brazyiak from his clutches.

"Blood, you done fucked up tha whole Gangsta Blood card wit' yo' petty bullshit! You feedin' otha niggas' hoods and lettin' tha westside homies starve and be dusty! It ain't gon be no mo' of that shit, Blood. Straight up! I'm tellin' all y'all niggas today that Lil Bick Back ain't speakin' for me or no other Gangsta Bloods in here, westside OR eastside, and if niggas got a problem wit' it, I need the fade right now!"

Brazyiak is known as a killer and fighter. The swelling up of Lil Bick Back's face lets everyone know that they will have a fight on their hands opposing Brazyiak in combat. The Bloods stand silent.

"That's what tha fuck I thought! Check this out, OG Big Red! You got the most niggas in here and you been lettin' all this Crab activity go on amongst tha Bloods so I'm holdin' you responsible, too, Blood!"

Brazyiak takes off on OG Big Red. OG Big Red grabs Brazyiak's entire body and slams him to the floor. He then puts his knee into Brazyiak's back as he lies semiconscious on the ground.

"Look, lil nigga! I respect yo' G! You da only nigga in here foolish enough to test me, Blood! So I am not gon' crack yo' got damn skull open but I'm callin da shots up in here now, Blood!"

Even with OG Big Red's massive weight on top of him and going in and out of consciousness, Brazyiak resists, "Blood! Fuck you!"

OG Big Red knocks Brazyiak out cold with a solid right punch.

"Lil Mousey! Blood, come ova here and get yo' homie! When Blood recova, we gon' speak on tha peckin' order in here."

Lil Mousey and a homie from Westside Gangsta Bloods pick up Brazyiak's bloodied and battered body and move him back to their section of the holding tank. Even though he was defeated physically, Brazyiak has won the respect of every Blood in the holding tank who witnessed him stand up to OG Big Red today. He is in the beginning stages of shifting power of the Bloods back to the Blood Alliance.

As he comes to, Lil Mousey is putting a towel on his face to bring down some of the swelling from his injuries sustained fighting OG Big Red earlier. He tries to open his right eye, but it still hurts too much. He tries to focuses it and sees a blurry figure standing before him.

"Soo Whoop! West Gang Blood!"

"Bountry! Blood!"

The two relatives embrace each other and Bountry sits down next to his big cousin. "Blood. I just found out it was you that got molly whooped by OG Big Red!"

"Ha-ha, lil nigga! I bet you didn't hear about me takin' off on Blood?"

"I did. Niggas said you hit him first but it wuz all downhill from there, Blood!"

Brazyiak laughs and spits blood out of his mouth.

"I'm glad to see you alive, Cuz! I figured you would have made it out of town and headed back to Cashville once the Feds came in!"

"Hell naw, Blood! As soon as da Feds locked da

westside down, they started comin' after all da big eastside gangs next. Niggas cracked me on imperial in the hood! Now you was ova there wit' tha east homies? How niggas been treatin' you, Blood?"

"Blood, it's all love! Niggas respect me outta respectin' you! But the set is all fucked up. Lil Bick Back been kissin' OG Big Red ass and its been hard for the homies on the westside in here."

"Yeah Mousey put me on to what was hattenin' befo' I got in tha tank, but all that shit is in tha past, Blood! That's why I fought big Blood Day One! We finna get the BA back brackin' in here, Blood, and I'm gon' need you to have my back rellie!"

"Blood! You know I gotcha muthafuckin' back!"

"That's what a nigga want to hear! Now go get me some more muthafuckin' towels so I can get my face right! We gon' have to go talk to OG Big Red and get this program on!"

Brazyiak has taken enough time nursing his wounds and he is as healed as much as he is going to be for the moment. He grabs Lil Mousey and Bountry and walks over to the PJ Bloods section of the holding cell to talk to OG Big Red. OG Big Red is in the middle of a workout routine and is covered in sweat. He grabs a towel from one of his underlings and wipes his face and tree trunk sized arms.

"What you back for some more whoop ass, Blood?"

Brazyiak stands right in front of OG Big Red. "Naw, Blood! I came over here to talk to you on the program in here wit' tha Bloods and me and you!"

OG Big Red continues wiping sweat from his brow and then throws the towel on the floor. "Blood, da program in here is PJ Bloods, den everybody else Blood. We da thickest in here, so we run da cell!"

"I hear you, but we gon' have to come to some betta terms on how tha otha Blood sets is treated in here! On Bloods, you know niggas ain't been doin' tha rest of tha Bloods right in here, OG Big Red. I know most niggas in here don't give a fuck and it's each man fo' self but I been pushin' this BA line and I know there is strength in numbas, Blood!"

"So what you sayin, YG?"

Brazyiak moves in very close to OG Big Red. He whispers the rest into his ear. "Blood, Damu is safe on tha outside and he will get me anything I need in here. I'm gon' put money on every B Dog books in here! I'm gon' put an extra twenty percent on any nigga that you fucks wit' and an extra fifty percent on yours, Blood! I'm also willin' to take care of any phone time and wrap up any bidness that need to be taken care of on tha outside for you or any Blood in tha can! But to do all that, niggas is gon' have to get in line wit' tha BA! We gon' have to be more organized and run the program right in here. Y'all niggas just been in here beastin' on each other. We gotta get ready for tha Feds and for tha Rips and I wanna shape the card up, Blood!"

OG Big Red stares in front of him. He shakes his head in agreement thinking of the possibilities of the benefits that

Brazyiak has offered him. "It sound good to me Blood, but you gonna be held accountable for all BA bidness, not me!"

Brazyiak looks OG Red straight in his eyes and says, "I'm wit' that, Blood!"

"Okay then, Blood, put yo' plan in motion and we can make it happen! But I need to let you know what's up on all the politics in here and how I been runnin' thangs!"

"Run it down to me, Blood!"

"I only fuck wit' one guard on payroll. His name is Peterson and he comes in on the night-shift. Blood will do anything you need him to do 'cuz his Pops is a Piru from Bompton and he puts me up on everythang comin' into da system from da Feds! We keep our knives wit' Blood, too. He brangs 'em in and takes 'em out at the end of his shift. Niggas ain't needed to stab nobody yet, but you never know, Blood. He also sends kites ova to the Crip cell fo' us. I keep lines open with tha shotcallas over there in case we need to get a nigga or vice versa."

"That's good to know. I need to know if a Crab from Kid Titties comes in named J Loc. I need that nigga stuck tha fuck up, Blood!"

"Shit, that shouldn't be no problem, Blood! I will put dat kite out on him now."

"Aight, Blood, I'm gon' get on the line wit' Damu and let him know how shit is movin' inside."

"Shit sound straight, Blood!"

As Brazyiak and the homies head back over to his section of the holding tank, OG Red yells out to him, "Blood, it was a young nigga from ESB that said he was your homie that got at one of my YGs on da outside on some type of bidness y'all had. He was checkin' to see if you was in here a while back to get wit' you. I'm gon' get at the young homie and run dat kite back to you, Blood!"

"That's what it is Blood. Just let me know!"

19

THE WRAP UP

In Mid City at J Loc's grandma's house, J Loc is out on bail after turning himself in and trying to figure out where his new life is heading. Karla has come to town to visit and the two lovebirds get a chance to see what actually being in the same city is like.

Karla is watching TV with J Loc in the room. Karla asks "Can we go to this party tonight at the Hotel Montage in Hollywood?"

J Loc, who was reading about a trade school on the internet, is distracted, "Hotel what? Yeah sure, whatever you want."

At the Four Seasons in Beverly Hills, Cold Hand Tony is laying up in a room with both his hoes, Cindy and Anna. They watch a reality show on TV, eat room service, smoke blunts, and talk shit. But something is different about Cindy, and she appears to now be playing the role of neglected bottom bitch but with high spirits. Tony is looking at her a bit skeptical, but is too happy by the sudden attitude change and the peace it has brought to their small family to investigate.

Tony starts to speak coughing on the blunt, "Yo! Ladies, start to get yourselves ready. You know there is that big NBA baller party at Hotel Montage tonight, so let's get both of you looking as sexy as possible and go up there and take all that money." Tony is a little drunk and feeling himself, but why shouldn't he be? His pimping game is paying bills and they are chilling in Beverly Hills. The girls exit the room to get ready.

■————————————————————————————■

Meanwhile in Inglewood at The Bottoms, Damu is meeting with more Blood leaders trying to strengthen the Blood Alliance when his cell rings. He answers and it's Councilman Lopez. "Damu, can you meet me at the Hotel Montage tonight at 10?"

"Yup."

■————————————————————————————■

Karla and J Loc step out of valet and there and head toward the guest list girl in front of the ropes. Before J Loc can say anything, Karla blurts out, "Karla K, plus one," and the door girl quickly whips out VIP bracelets and puts them on J Loc and Karla.

J Loc grins, a little taken aback but playing it cool. "So you've been in LA a week and your big balling with all the hookups?"

Karla sees where he going and gets right to the point. "Look here, nigga, you wasn't calling a bitch for months! You think a bitch as fine as me sits around waiting? Hell naw! I have a gang of friends who want to kick it, but to be real, I want to fuck with you, but I'm gon' keep it completely 100 with you. When you were tripping I was acting single, and if you start tripping again, I will go right back."

J Loc is pissed off at her tirade, but he continues to play it cool at the club and with tons of folks around, he decides to fall back. They walk to the bar and J Loc buys them each a drink. As they walk into the VIP section, some NBA player spots Karla. "What up, Karla K?"

Karla smiles and plays the Hollywood role as she introduces J Loc to her NBA pals. After the quick intro, J Loc has had about all he can take and he pulls Karla to the side. "I thought you was a down type broad, but with all this Hollywood shit, kicking it with NBA muthafuckas, I see what type of broad you are. You're just a groupie type bitch!"

Karla is enraged and as she storms off, she says, "Fuck you, nigga!"

At the entrance, CHT and his two hoes walk in to the party. They are quite a sight, Anna with her model good looks and huge tits and Cindy with that phat black girl ass on a white girl. They both had on super skimpy clothes and were getting gawked from all sides. CHT gets a table and he and Anna sit down. Cindy goes to the bathroom and practically bumps into a heated J Loc, who was heading for the door.

On first glance, Cindy is smitten on the good looking thug J Loc and when J Loc see's Cindy's huge ass, his anger is forgotten and he kicks into player mode. "Oh baby, I'm sorry! I didn't mean to bump into you. Can I get you a drink to make up for it?" Cindy lustfully looks J Loc up and down as they head to the bar.

In the VIP section, CHT is introducing Councilman Lopez to Anna, and Lopez doesn't even attempt to hide his lustful thoughts. CHT leaves them to get acquainted and start his meeting with Damu. But CHT is also looking for Cindy as Anna already has a huge mark she is starting to work and he wants to make sure Cindy is doing the same.

When he walks up on Cindy hanging off of J Loc at the bar, he is immediately pissed. J Loc doesn't look like any kind of mark. With all this money in the room, Cindy is over here fucking with this thug dude. But CHT holds it down and turns on his smooth player mode. However, Cindy ain't buying it and she flips out. "You wack ass fake pimp, I'm done with your broke ass!"

CHT explodes, "What bitch? You think you gonna leave me to go fuck this gangbanger nigga out in..." but before he even finishes the sentence, J Loc socks him and knock him out cold.

Chaos ensues in the club as some other cats accidently got bumped, and before you know it, the whole club has exploded into a major brawl with chairs flyin', glass breakin', bitches hollerin', and all that bidness.

To Be Continued...

Author TK Kimbro *aka* TK Black has worked as a manager, A&R, radio promoter, and label executive. He is the founder of the brand strategy and management firm The Synergy Group LA and contributes as a writer to several online blogs. He volunteers for the National Kidney Foundation and does community outreach through public speaking.

more titles from

BOOKS

www.ingramcontent.com/pod-product-compliance
Lightning Source LLC
Chambersburg PA
CBHW022045240626
47154CB00007B/2571